Our Lady of Darkness

From his window there thrust itself a pale brown thing that wildly waved its long, uplifted arms at him. While low between them he could see its face stretched toward him, a mask as narrow as a ferret's, a pale brown utterly blank triangle, two points above that might mean eyes or ears, and one ending below in a tapered chin . . . no, snout . . . no, very short trunk—*a questing mouth that looked as if it were for sucking marrow. Then the paramental entity reached through the glasses at his eyes . . .*

"AN EXTRAORDINARY CHILLER SO SUBTLY WRITTEN THAT THE EXISTENCE OF DEMONS BECOMES ACTUALLY CONVINCING."

—*The Oregonian*

"CERTAINLY A MAJOR HORROR NOVEL. THE SLOW STEADY BUILD TO A MOMENT OF SUPREME HORROR WILL LEAVE READERS ABSOLUTELY SCREAMING WITH FRIGHT . . . WILL STAND AS AN UNRIVALED HORROR CLASSIC!"

—*Delap's Fantasy and Science Fiction Review*

OUR LADY OF DARKNESS

FRITZ LEIBER

ACE FANTASY BOOKS
NEW YORK

This Ace Fantasy Book contains the complete
text of the original hardcover edition.
It has been completely reset in a typeface
designed for easy reading, and was printed
from new film.

OUR LADY OF DARKNESS

An Ace Fantasy Book / published by arrangement with
the author's agent

PRINTING HISTORY
Berkley-Putnam edition / 1977
Berkley edition / February 1978
Ace edition / April 1984

ISBN: 0-441-64417-1

Ace Fantasy Books are published by The Berkley Publishing Group,
200 Madison Avenue, New York, New York 10016.
PRINTED IN THE UNITED STATES OF AMERICA

But the third Sister, who is also the youngest—! Hush! whisper whilst we talk of *her*! Her kingdom is not large, or else no flesh should live; but within that kingdom all power is hers. Her head, turreted like that of Cybele, rises almost beyond the reach of sight. She droops not; and her eyes, rising so high, *might* be hidden by distance. But, being what they are, they cannot be hidden; through the treble veil of crape which she wears the fierce light of a blazing misery, that rests not for matins or for vespers, for noon of day or noon of night, for ebbing or for flowing tide, may be read from the very ground. She is the defier of God. She also is the mother of lunacies, and the suggestress of suicides. Deep lie the roots of her power; but narrow is the nation that she rules. For she can approach only those in whom a profound nature has been upheaved by central convulsions; in whom the heart trembles and the brain rocks under conspiracies of tempest from without and tempest from within. Madonna moves with uncertain steps, fast or slow, but still with tragic grace. Our Lady of Sighs creeps timidly and stealthily. But this youngest Sister moves with incalculable motions, bounding, and with tiger's leaps. She carries no key; for, though coming rarely amongst men, she storms all doors at which she is permitted to enter at all. And *her* name is *Mater Tenebrarum*—our Lady of Darkness.

——Thomas De Quincy
        "Levana and Our Three Ladies of Sorrow"

Suspiria de Profundis

1

THE SOLITARY, steep hill called Corona Heights was black as pitch and very silent, like the heart of the unknown. It looked steadily downward and northeast away at the nervous, bright lights of downtown San Francisco as if it were a great predatory beast of night surveying its territory in patient search of prey.

The waxing gibbous moon had set, and the stars at the top of the black heavens were still diamond sharp. To the west lay a low bank of fog. But to the east, beyond the city's business center and the fog-surfaced Bay, the narrow ghostly ribbon of the dawn's earliest light lay along the tops of the low hills behind Berkeley, Oakland, and Alameda, and still more distant Devil's Mountain— Mount Diablo.

On every side of Corona Heights the street and house lights of San Francisco, weakest at end of night, hemmed it in apprehensively, as if it were indeed a dangerous animal. But on the hill itself there was not a single light. An observer below would have found it almost impossible to make out its jagged spine and the weird crags crowning its top (which even the gulls avoided); and breaking out here and there from its raw, barren sides, which although sometimes touched by fog, had not known the pelting of rain for months.

Someday the hill might be bulldozed down, when greed had grown even greater than it is today and awe of primeval nature even less, but now it could still awaken panic terror.

Too savage and cantankerous for a park, it was inade-

quately designated as a playground. True, there were
some tennis courts and limited fields of grass and low
buildings and little stands of thick pine around its base;
but above those it rose rough, naked, and contemptuously
aloof.

And now something seemed to stir in the massed darkness there. (Hard to tell what.) Perhaps one or more of the
city's wild dogs, homeless for generations, yet able to
pass as tame. (In a big city, if you see a dog going about
his business, menacing no one, fawning on no one, fus-
sing at no one—in fact, behaving like a good citizen with
work to do and no time for nonsense—and if that dog
lacks tag or collar, then you may be sure he hasn't a
neglectful owner, but is wild—and well adjusted.)
Perhaps some wilder and more secret animal that had
never submitted to man's rule, yet lived almost un-
glimpsed amongst him. Perhaps, conceivably, a man (or
woman) so sunk in savagery or psychosis that he (or she)
didn't need light. Or perhaps only the wind.

And now the eastern ribbon grew dark red, the whole
sky lightened from the east toward the west, the stars were
fading, and Corona Heights began to show its raw, dry,
pale brown surface.

Yet the impression lingered that the hill had grown
restless, having at last decided on its victim.

2

Two hours later, Franz Westen looked out of his open casement window at the 1,000-foot TV tower rising bright red and white in the morning sunlight out of the snowy fog that still masked Sutro Crest and Twin Peaks three miles away and against which Corona Heights stood out, humped and pale brown. The TV tower—San Francisco's Eiffel, you could call it—was broad-shouldered, slender-waisted, and long-legged like a beautiful and stylish woman—or demigoddess. It mediated between Franz and the universe these days, just as man is supposed to mediate between the atoms and the stars. Looking at it, admiring, almost reverencing it, was his regular morning greeting to the universe, his affirmation that they were in touch, before making coffee and settling back into bed with clipboard and pad for the day's work of writing supernatural horror stories and especially (his bread and butter) novelizing the TV program "Weird Underground," so that the mob of viewers could also read, if they wanted to, something like the mélange of witchcraft, Watergate, and puppy love they watched on the tube. A year or so ago he would have been focusing inward on his miseries at this hour and worrying about the day's first drink—whether he still had it or had drunk up everything last night—but that was in the past, another matter.

Faint, dismal foghorns cautioned each other in the distance. Franz's mind darted briefly two miles behind him to where more fog would be blanketing San Francisco Bay except for the four tops thrusting from it of the first

span of the bridge to Oakland. Under that frosty-looking
surface there would be the ribbons of impatient, fuming
cars, the talking ships, and coming from far below the
water and the mucky bottom, but heard by fishermen in
little boats, the eerie roar of the BART (Bay Area Rapid
Transit) trains rocketing through the tube as they carried
the main body of commuters to their jobs.

Dancing up the sea air into his room there came the gay,
sweet notes of a Telemann minuet blown by Cal from her
recorder two floors below. She meant them for him, he
told himself, even though he was twenty years older. He
looked at the oil portrait of his dead wife Daisy over the
studio bed, beside a drawing of the TV tower in spidery
black lines on a large oblong of fluorescent red cardboard,
and felt no guilt. Three years of drunken grief—a record
wake!—had worked that all away, ending almost exactly
a year ago.

His gaze dropped to the studio bed, still half-unmade.
On the undisturbed half, nearest the wall, there stretched
out a long, colorful scatter of magazines, science-fiction
paperbacks, a few hardcover detective novels still in their
wrappers, a few bright napkins taken home from restaurants, and a half-dozen of those shiny little *Golden Guides*
and *Knowledge Through Color* books—his recreational
reading as opposed to his working materials and references arranged on the coffee table beside the bed. They'd
been his chief—almost his sole—companions during the
three years he'd laid sodden there stupidly goggling at the
TV across the room; but always fingering them and
stupefiedly studying their bright, easy pages from time to
time. Only a month ago it had suddenly occurred to him
that their gay casual scatter added up to a slender, carefree
woman lying beside him on top of the covers—that was
why he never put them on the floor; why he contented
himself with half the bed; why he unconsciously arranged
them in a female form with long, long legs. They were a
"scholar's mistress," he decided, on the analogy of
"Dutch wife," that long, slender bolster sleepers clutch
to soak up sweat in tropical countries—a very secret

playmate, a dashing but studious call girl, a slim, incestuous sister, eternal comrade of his writing work.

With an affectionate glance toward his oil-painted dead wife and a keen, warm thought toward Cal still sending up pirouetting notes on the air, he said softly with a conspiratorial smile to the slender cubist form occupying all the inside of the bed, "Don't worry, dear, you'll always be my best girl, though we'll have to keep it a deep secret from the others," and turned back to the window.

It was the TV tower standing way out there so modern-tall on Sutro Crest, its three long legs still deep in fog, that had first gotten him hooked on reality again after his long escape in drunken dream. At the beginning the tower had seemed unbelievably cheap and garish to him, an intrusion worse than the high rises in what had been the most romantic of cities, an obscene embodiment of the blatant world of sales and advertising—even, with its great red and white limbs against blue sky (as now, above the fog), an emblazonment of the American flag in its worst aspects: barberpole stripes; fat, flashy, regimented stars. But then it had begun to impress him against his will with its winking red lights at night—so many of them! he had counted nineteen: thirteen steadies and six winkers—and then it had subtly led his interest to the other distances in the cityscape and also in the real stars so far beyond, and on lucky nights the moon, until he had got passionately interested in all real things again, no matter what. And the process had never stopped; it still kept on. Until Saul had said to him, only the other day, "I don't know about welcoming in every new reality. You could run into a bad customer."

"That's fine talk, coming from a nurse in a psychiatric ward," Gunnar had said, while Franz had responded instantly, "Taken for granted. Concentration camps. Germs of plague."

"I don't mean things like those exactly," Saul had said. "I guess I mean the sort of things some of my guys run into at the hospital."

"But those would be hallucinations, projections,

archetypes, and so on, wouldn't they?'' Franz had observed, a little wonderingly. "Parts of *inner* reality, of course.''

''Sometimes I'm not so sure,'' Saul had said slowly. ''Who's going to know what's what if a crazy says he's just seen a ghost? Inner or outer reality? Who's to tell then? What do you say, Gunnar, when one of your computers starts giving readouts it shouldn't?''

''That it's got overheated,'' Gun had answered with conviction. ''Remember, my computers are normal people to start out with, not weirdos and psychotics like your guys.''

''Normal—what's that?'' Saul had countered.

Franz had smiled at his two friends who occupied two apartments on the floor between his and Cal's. Cal had smiled, too, though not so much.

Now he looked out the window again. Just outside it, the six-story drop went down past Cal's window—a narrow shaft between this building and the next, the flat roof of which was about level with his floor. Just beyond that, framing his view to either side, were the bone-white, rain-stained back walls—mostly windowless—of two high rises that went up and up.

It was a rather narrow slot between them, but through it he could see all of reality he needed to keep in touch. And if he wanted more he could always go up two stories to the roof, which he often did these days and nights.

From this building low on Nob Hill the sea of roofs went down and down, then up and up again, tinying with distance, to the bank of fog now masking the dark green slope of Sutro Crest and the bottom of the tripod TV tower. But in the middle distance a shape like a crouching beast, pale brown in the morning sunlight, rose from the sea of roofs. The map called it just Corona Heights. It had been teasing Franz's curiosity for several weeks. Now he focused his small seven-power Nikon binoculars on its bare earth slopes and humped spine, which stood out sharply against the white fog. He wondered why it hadn't been built up. Big cities certainly had some strange intrusions in them. This one was like a raw remnant of upthrust from the earthquake of 1906, he told himself, smiling at the unscientific fancy. Could it be called Corona Heights from the crown of irregularly clumped big rocks on its top, he asked himself, as he rotated the knurled knob a little more, and they came out momentarily sharp and clear against the fog.

A rather thin, pale brown rock detached itself from the others and waved at him. Damn the way these glasses jiggled with his heartbeat! A person who expected to see neat, steady pictures through them just hadn't used binoculars. Or could it be a floater in his vision, a microscopic speck in the eye's fluid? No, there he had it again! Just as he'd thought, it was some tall person in a long raincoat or drab robe moving about almost as if dancing. You couldn't see human figures in any detail at two miles even with sevenfold magnification; you just got a general impression of movements and attitude. They were simplified. This skinny figure on Corona Heights was moving around rather rapidly, all right, maybe dancing with arms waving high, but that was the most you could tell.

As he lowered the binoculars he smiled broadly at the thought of some hippie type greeting the morning sun with ritual prancings on a mid-city hilltop newly emerged from fog. And with chantings too, no doubt, if one could hear—unpleasant wailing ululations like the yelping siren he heard now in the distance, the sort that was frantic-making when heard too close. Someone from the Haight-Ashbury, likely, it was out that way. A stoned priest of a modern sun god dancing around an accidental high-set Stonehenge. The thing had given him a start, at first, but now he found it very amusing.

A sudden wind blew in. Should he shut the window? No, for now the air was quiet again. It had just been a freakish gust.

He set down the binoculars on his desk beside two thin old books. The topmost, bound in dirty gray, was open at its title page, which read in a utilitarian typeface and layout marking it as last century's—a grimy job by a grimy printer with no thought of artistry: *Megapoliso-mancy: A New Science of Cities*, by Thibaut de Castries. Now that was a funny coincidence! He wondered if a drug-crazed priest in earthen robes—or a dancing rock, for that matter!—would have been recognized by that strange old crackpot Thibaut as one of the "secret occurrences" he had predicted for big cities in the solemnly straight-faced book he'd written back in the 1890s. Franz told himself that he must read some more in it, and in the other book, too.

But not right now, he told himself suddenly, looking back at the coffee table where there reposed, on top of a large and heavy manila envelope already stamped and addressed to his New York agent, the typed manuscript of his newest novelization—*Weird Underground #7: Towers of Treason*—all ready to go except for one final descriptive touch he'd hankered to check on and put in; he liked to give his readers their money's worth, even though this series was the flimsiest of escape reading, secondary creativity on his part at best.

But this time, he told himself, he'd send the novelization off without the final touch and declare today a holiday—he was beginning to get an idea of what he wanted to do with it. With only a flicker of guilt at the thought of cheating his readers of a trifle, he got dressed and made himself a cup of coffee to carry down to Cal's, and as afterthoughts the two thin old books under his arm (he wanted to show them to Cal) and the binoculars in his jacket pocket—just in case he was tempted to check up again on Corona Heights and its freaky rock god.

3

IN THE HALL, Franz passed the black knobless door of the disused broom closet and the smaller padlocked one of an old laundry chute or dumbwaiter (no one remembered which) and the big gilded one of the elevator with the strange black window beside it, and he descended the red-carpeted stairs, which between each floor went in right-angling flights of six and three and six steps around the oblong stair well beneath the dingy skylight two stories up from his floor. He didn't stop at Gun's and Saul's floor—the next, the fifth—though he glanced at both their doors, which were diagonally opposite each other near the stairs, but kept on to the fourth.

At each landing he glimpsed more of the strange black vindows that couldn't be opened and a few more black doors without knobs in the empty red-carpeted halls. It was odd how old buildings had secret spaces in them that weren't really hidden but were never noticed; like this one's five airshafts, the windows to which had been painted black at some time to hide their dinginess, and the disused broom closets, which had lost their function with the passing of cheap maid service, and in the baseboard the tightly snap-capped round openings of a vacuum system which surely hadn't been used for decades. He doubted anyone in the building ever consciously saw them, except himself, newly aroused to reality by the tower and all. Today they made him think for a moment of the old times when this building had probably been a small hotel with monkey-faced bellboys and maids whom his fancy pictured as French with short skirts and naughty low

laughs (dour slatterns more likely, reason commented).
He knocked at 407.

It was one of those times when Cal looked like a serious
schoolgirl of seventeen, lightly wrapped in dreams, and
not ten years older, her actual age. Long, dark hair, blue
eyes, a quiet smile. They'd been to bed together twice, but
didn't kiss now—it might have seemed presumptuous on
his part, she didn't quite offer to, and in any case he
wasn't sure how far he wanted to commit himself. She
invited him in to the breakfast she was making. Though a
duplicate of his, her room looked much nicer—too good
for the building—she had redecorated it completely with
help from Gunnar and Saul. Only it didn't have a view.
There was a music stand by the window and an electronic
piano that was mostly keyboard and black box and that
had earphones for silent practicing, as well as speaker.

"I came down because I heard you blowing the Telemann," Franz said.

"Perhaps I did it to summon you," Cal replied off-
handedly from where she was busy with the hot plates and
toaster. "There's magic in music, you know."

"You're thinking of *The Magic Flute?*" he asked.
"You make a recorder sound like one."

"There's magic in all woodwinds," she assured him.
"Mozart's supposed to have changed the plot of *The
Magic Flute* midway so that it wouldn't be too close to
that of a rival opera, *The Enchanted Bassoon.*"

He laughed, then went on. "Musical notes do have at
least one supernatural power. They can levitate, fly up
through the air. Of course words can do that, too, but not
as well."

"How do you figure that?" she asked over her
shoulder.

"From cartoons and comic strips," he told her.
"Words need balloons to hold them up, but notes just
come flying out of the piano or whatever."

"They have those little black wings," she said, "at
least the eighth and shorter ones. But it's all true. Music

can fly—it's all release—and it has the power to release other things and make them fly and swirl.''

He nodded. "I wish you'd release the notes of this piano, though, and let them swirl out when you practice harpsichord,'' he said, looking at the electronic instrument, "instead of keeping them shut up inside the earphones.''

"You'd be the only one who'd like it," she informed him.

"There's Gun and Saul," he said.

"Their rooms aren't on this shaft. Besides, you'd get sick of scales and arpeggios yourself.''

"I'm not so sure," he said, then teased, "But maybe harpsichord notes are too tinkly to make magic.''

"I hate that word," she said, "but you're still wrong. Tinkly (ugh!) notes can make magic too. Remember Papageno's bells—there's more than one kind of magic music in *The Flute*.''

They ate toast, juice, and eggs. Franz told Cal of his decision to send the manuscript of *Towers of Treason* off just as it was.

He finished, "So my readers won't find out just what a document-shredding machine sounds like when it works—what difference does that make? I actually saw that program on the tube, but when the Satanist wizard fed in the rune, they had smoke come out—which seemed stupid.''

"I'm glad to hear you say that," she said sharply. "You put too much effort into rationalizing that silly program." Her expression changed. "Still, I don't know. It's partly that you always try to do your best, whatever at, that makes me think of you as a professional.'' She smiled.

He felt another faint twinge of guilt but fought it down easily.

While she was pouring him more coffee, he said, "I've got a great idea. Let's go to Corona Heights today. I think there'd be a great view of Downtown and the Inner Bay.

We could take the Muni most of the way, and there shouldn't be too much climbing.''

"You forget I've got to practice for the concert tomorrow night and couldn't risk my hands, in any case," she said a shade reproachfully. "But don't let that stop you," she added with a smile that asked his pardon. "Why not ask Gun or Saul—I think they're off today. Gun's great on climbing. Where is Corona Heights?''

He told her, remembering that her interest in Frisco was neither as new nor as passionate as his—he had a convert's zeal.

"That must be close to Buena Vista Park," she said. "Now don't go wandering in there, please. There've been some murders there quite recently. Drug related. The other side of Buena Vista is right up against the Haight.''

"I don't intend to," he said, "though maybe you're a little too uptight about the Haight. It's quieted down a lot the last few years. Why, I got these two books there in one of those really fabulous secondhand stores.''

"Oh, yes, you were going to show them to me," she said.

He handed her the one that had been open, saying, "That's just about the most fascinating book of pseudo-science I've ever seen—it has some genuine insights mixed with the hokum. No date, but printed about 1900, I'd judge.''

" 'Megapolisomancy,' " she pronounced carefully. "Now what would that be? Telling the future from . . . from cities?''

"From *big* cities," he said, nodding.

"Oh, yes, the *mega*.''

He went on. "Telling the future and all other sorts of things. And apparently making magic, too, from that knowledge. Though de Castries calls it a 'new science,' as if he were a second Galileo. Anyhow, this de Castries is very much concerned about the 'vast amounts' of steel and paper that are being accumulated in big cities. And coal oil (kerosene) and natural gas. And electricity, too, if you can believe it—he carefully figures out just how much

electricity is in how many thousands of miles of wire, how
many tons of illuminating gas in tanks, how much steel in
the new skyscrapers, how much paper for government
records and yellow journalism, and so on.''

"My-oh-my," Cal commented. "I wonder what he'd
think if he were alive today."

"His direst predictions vindicated, no doubt. He *did*
speculate about the growing menace of automobiles and
gasoline, but especially electric cars carrying buckets of
direct electricity around in batteries. He came so close to
anticipating our modern concern about pollution—he
even talks of 'the vast congeries of gigantic fuming vats'
of sulphuric acid needed to manufacture steel. But what
he was most agitated about was the psychological or
spiritual (he calls them 'paramental') effects of all that
stuff accumulating in big cities, its sheer liquid and solid
mass."

"A real proto-hippie," Cal put it. "What sort of man
was he? Where did he live? What else did he do?"

"There's absolutely no indication in the book of any of
those things," Franz told her, "and I've never turned up
another reference to him. In his book he refers to New
England and eastern Canada quite a bit, and New York
City, but only in a general way. He also mentioned Paris
(he had it in for the Eiffel Tower) and France a few times.
And Egypt."

Cal nodded. "What's with the other book?"

"Something quite interesting," Franz said, passing it
over. "As you can see, it's not a regular book at all but a
journal of blank rice-paper pages, as thin as onionskin but
more opaque, bound in ribbed silk that was tea rose, I'd
say, before it faded. The entries, in violet ink with a fine-
point fountain pen, I'd guess, hardly go a quarter of the
way through. The rest of the pages are blank. Now when I
bought these books they were tied together with an old
piece of string. They looked as if they'd been joined for
decades—you can still see the marks."

"Uh-huh," Cal agreed. "Since 1900 or so? A very
charming diary book—I'd like to have one like it."

"Yes, isn't it? No, just since 1928. A couple of the entries are dated, and they all seem to have been made in the space of a few weeks."

"Was he a poet?" Cal asked. "I see groups of indented lines. Who was he, anyway? Old de Castries?"

"No, not de Castries, though someone who had read his book and knew him. But I do think he was a poet. In fact, I think I have identified the writer, though it's not easy to prove since he nowhere signs himself. I think he was Clark Ashton Smith."

"I've heard that name," Cal said.

"Probably from me," Franz told her. "He was another supernatural horror writer. Very rich, doomful stuff: Arabian Nights chinoiserie. A mood like Beddoes's *Death's Jest-Book*. He lived near San Francisco and knew the old artistic crew, he visited George Sterling at Carmel, and he could easily have been here in San Francisco in 1928 when he'd just begun to write his finest stories. I've given a photocopy of that journal to Jaime Donaldus Byers, who's an authority on Smith and who lives here on Beaver Street (which is just by Corona Heights, by the way, the map shows it), and he showed it to de Camp (who thinks it's Smith for sure) and to Roy Squires (who's as sure it isn't). Byers himself just can't decide, says there's no evidence for an extended San Francisco trip by Smith then, and that although the writing looks like Smith's, it's more agitated than any he's ever seen. But I have reasons to think Smith would have kept the trip secret and have had cause to be supremely agitated."

"Oh, my," Cal said. "You've gone to a lot of trouble and thought about it. But I can see why. It's *très romantique*, just the feel of this ribbed silk and rice paper."

"I had a special reason," Franz said, unconsciously dropping his voice a little. "I bought the books four years ago, you see, before I moved here, and I read a lot in the journal. The violet-ink person (whoever, *I* think Smith) keeps writing about 'visiting Tiberius at 607 Rhodes.' In fact, the journal is entirely—or chiefly—an account of a series of such interviews. That '607 Rhodes' stuck in my

mind, so that when I went hunting a cheaper place to live
and was shown the room here—''

"Of course, it's your apartment number, 607," Cal
interrupted.

Franz nodded. "I got the idea it was predestined, or
prearranged in some mysterious way. As if I'd had to look
for the '607 Rhodes' and had found it. I had a lot of
mysterious drunken ideas in those days and didn't always
know what I was doing or where I was—for instance, I've
forgotten exactly where the fabulous store was where I
bought these books, and its name, if it had one. In fact, I
was pretty drunk most of the time—period.''

"You certainly were," Cal agreed, "though in a quiet
way. Saul and Gun and I wondered about you and we
pumped Dorotea Luque and Bonita," she added, refer-
ring to the Peruvian apartment manager and her thirteen-
year-old daughter. "Even then you didn't seem an ordinary lush. Dorotea said you wrote '*ficción* to scare, about
espectros y fantasmas de los muertos y las muertas,' but
that she thought you were a gentleman.''

Franz laughed. "Specters and phantoms of dead men
and dead ladies. How very Spanish! Still, I'll bet you
never thought—'' he began and stopped.

"That I'd some day get into bed with you?" Cal finished for him. "Don't be too sure. I've always had erotic
fantasies about older men. But tell me—how did your
weird then-brain fit in the Rhodes part?"

"It never did," Franz confessed. "Though I still think
the violet-ink person had some definite place in mind,
besides the obvious reference to Tiberius's exile by Au-
gustus to the island of Rhodes, where the Roman em-
peror-to-be studied oratory along with sexual perversion
and a spot of witchcraft. The violet-ink person doesn't
always say Tiberius, incidentally. It's sometimes
Theobald and sometimes Tybalt, and once it's Thrasyllus,
who was Tiberius's personal fortuneteller and sorcerer.
But always there's that '607 Rhodes.' And once it's
Theudebaldo and once Dietbold, but three times Thibaut,
which is what makes me sure, besides all the other things,

it must have been de Castries that Smith was visiting almost every day and writing about.''

''Franz,'' Cal said, ''all this is perfectly fascinating, but I've just got to start practicing. Working up harpsichord on a dinky electronic piano is hard enough, and tomorrow night's not just anything, it's the Fifth Brandenburg Concerto.''

''I know, I'm sorry I forgot about it. It was inconsiderate of me, a male chauvinist—'' Franz began, getting to his feet.

''Now, don't get tragic,'' Cal said briskly. ''I enjoyed every minute, really, but now I've got to work. Here, take your cup—and for heaven's sake, these books—or I'll be peeking into them when I should be practicing. Cheer up—at least you're not a male chauvinist pig, you only ate one piece of toast.

''And—Franz,'' she called. He turned with his things at the door. ''Do be careful up there around Beaver and Buena Vista. Take Gun or Saul. And remember—'' Instead of saying what, she kissed two fingers and held them out toward him a moment, looking quite solemnly into his eyes.

He smiled, nodded twice, and went out feeling happy and excited. But as he closed the door behind him he decided that whether or not he went to Corona Heights, he wouldn't ask either of the two men on the next floor up to go with him—it was a question of courage, or at least independence. No, today would be his own adventure. Damn the torpedoes! Full speed ahead!

4

THE HALL OUTSIDE Cal's door duplicated all the features of
the one on Franz's floor: black-painted airshaft window,
knobless door to disused broom closet, drab golden
elevator door, and low-set, snap-capped vacuum outlet—
a relic of the days when the motor for a building's vacuum
system was in the basement and the maid handled only a
long hose and brush. But before Franz, starting down the
hall, had passed any of these, he heard from ahead an
intimate, giggly laugh that made him remember the one
he'd imagined for the imaginary maids. Then some words
he couldn't catch in a man's voice: low, rapid, and jocu-
lar. Saul's?—it did seem to come from above. Then the
feminine or girlish laughter again, louder and a little
explosive, almost as if someone were being tickled. Then
a rush of light footsteps coming down the stairs.

He reached them just in time to get a glimpse, down and
across the stairwell, of a shadowy slender figure disappearing around the last visible angle—just the suggestion
of black hair and clothing and slim white wrists and
ankles, all in swift movement. He moved to the well and
looked down it, struck by how the successive floors below
were like the series of reflections you saw when you stood
between two mirrors. The rapid footsteps continued their
spiraling descent all the way down, but whoever was
making them was keeping to the wall and away from the
rail lining the well, as if driven by centrifugal force, so he
got no further glimpses.

As he peered down that long, narrow tube dimly lit
from the skylight above, still thinking of the black-clad

17

limbs and the laughter, a murky memory rose in his mind
and for a few moments possessed him utterly. Although it
refused to come wholly clear, it gripped him with the
authority of a very unpleasant dream or bad drunk. He was
standing upright in a dark, claustrophobically narrow,
crowded, musty space. Through the fabric of his trousers
he felt a small hand laid on his genitals and he heard a low,
wicked laugh. He looked down in his memory and saw the
foreshortened, ghostly, featureless oval of a small face
and the laugh was repeated, mockingly. Somehow it
seemed there were black tendrils all around him. He felt a
weight of sick excitement and guilt and, almost, fear.

The murky memory lifted as Franz realized the figure
on the stairs had to have been that of Bonita Luque
wearing the black pajamas and robe and feathered black
mules she'd been handed down from her mother and
already outgrown, but sometimes still wore as she darted
around the building on her mother's early-morning er-
rands. He smiled disparagingly at the thought that he was
almost sorry (not really!) he was no longer drunk and so
able to nurse various kinky excitements.

He started up the stairs, but stopped almost at once
when he heard Gun's and Saul's voices from the floor
above. He did not want to see either of them now, at first
simply from a reluctance to share today's mood and plans
with anyone but Cal, but as he listened to the clear and
sharpening voices his motive became more complicated.

Gun asked, "What was that all about?"

Saul answered, "Her mother sent the kid up to check if
either of us had lost a cassette player-recorder. She thinks
her kleptomaniac on the second floor has one that doesn't
belong to her."

Gun remarked, "That's a big word for Mrs. Luque."

Saul said, "Oh, I suppose she said 'e-stealer.' I told the
kid that no, I still had mine."

Gun asked. "Why didn't Bonita check with me?"

Saul answered, "Because I told her you didn't have a
cassette player to start with. What's the matter? Feeling
left out?"

"No!"

During this interchange Gun's voice had grown increasingly nagging, Saul's progressively cooler yet also teasing. Franz had listened to mild speculation about the degree of homosexuality in Gun's and Saul's friendship, but this was the first time he found himself really wondering about it. No, he definitely didn't want to barge in now.

Saul persisted, "Then what's the matter? Hell, Gun, you know I always horse around with Bonny."

Gun's voice was almost waspish as he said, "I know I'm a puritanized North European, but I'd like to know just how far liberation from Anglo-Saxon body-contact taboos is supposed to go."

And Saul's voice was almost taunting as he replied, "Why, just as far as you both think proper, I suppose."

There was the sound of a door closing very deliberately. It was repeated. Then silence. Franz breathed his relief, continued softly up—and as he emerged into the fifth-floor hall found himself almost face to face with Gun, who was standing in front of the shut door to his room, glaring across at Saul's. Set on the floor beside him was a knee-high rectangular object with a chrome carrying handle protruding from its gray fabric cover.

Gunnar Nordgren was a tall, slim man, ashen blond, a fined-down Viking. Right now he had shifted his gaze and was looking at Franz with a growing embarrassment that matched Franz's own feelings. Abruptly Gun's usual amiability flooded back into his face, and he said, "Say, I'm glad you came by. A couple of nights ago you were wondering about document-shredding machines. Here's one I had here from the office overnight."

He whipped off the cover, revealing a tall blue and silvery box with a foot-wide maw on top and a red button. The maw fed down into a deep basket which Franz, coming closer, could see was one-quarter filled with a dirty snow of paper diamonds less than a quarter inch across.

The uncomfortable feelings of a moment before were gone. Looking up, Franz said, "I know you're going to work and all, but could I hear it in operation once?"

"Of course." Gun unlocked the door behind him and led Franz into a neat, rather sparely furnished room, the first features of which to strike the eye were large astronomical photographs in color and skiing equipment. As Gun unrolled the electric cord and plugged it in, he said lightheartedly, "This is a Shredbasket put out by Destroysit. Properly dire names, eh? Costs only five hundred dollars or so. Larger models go up to two thousand. A set of circular knives cuts the paper to ribbons; then another set cuts the ribbons across. Believe it or not, these machines were developed from ones for making confetti. I like that—it suggests that mankind first thinks of making frivolous things and only later puts them to serious use—if you can call this serious. Games before guilt."

The words poured out of him in such an excess of excitement or relief that Franz forgot his wonder as to why Gun should have brought such a machine home—what he'd been destroying. Gun continued, "The ingenious Italians—what was it Shakespeare said? Supersubtle Venetians?—lead the world, you know, in inventing machines for food and fun. Ice-cream makers, pasta extruders, espresso coffee machines, set-piece fireworks, hurdy-gurdies . . . and confetti. Well, here goes."

Franz had taken out a small notebook and ballpoint pen. As Gun's finger moved toward the red button, he leaned close, rather cautiously, expecting some rather loud sound.

Instead, there came a faint, breathy buzzing, as if Time were clearing her throat.

Delightedly Franz jotted down just that.

Gun fed in a pastel sheet. Pale blue snow showered down upon the dirty white. The sound barely thickened a little.

Franz thanked Gun and left him coiling up the cord. Mounting past his own floor and the seventh toward the roof, he felt pleased. Getting that scrap of observed fact had been just the bit of luck he'd needed to start the day perfectly.

5

THE CUBICAL ROOM housing the elevator's hoist was like a wizard's den atop a tower: skylight thickly filmed with dust, electric motor like a broad-shouldered dwarf in greasy green armor, and old-fashioned relays in the form of eight black cast-iron arms that writhed when in use like those of a chained-down giant spider—and with big copper switches that clashed loudly as they opened and closed whenever a button was pushed below, like such a spider's jaws.

Franz stepped out into sunlight on the flat, low-walled roof. Tar-embedded gravel gritted faintly under his shoes. The cool breeze was welcome.

To the east and north bulked the huge downtown buildings and whatever secret spaces they contained, blocking off the Bay. How old Thibaut would have scowled at the Transamerica Pyramid and the purple-brown Bank of America monster! Even at the new Hilton and St. Francis towers. The words came into his head, "The ancient Egyptians only buried people in their pyramids. We are living in ours." Now where had he read that? Why, in *Megapolisomancy*, of course. How apt! And did the modern pyramids have in them secret markings foretelling the future and crypts for sorcery?

He walked past the low-walled rectangular openings of the narrow airshafts lined with gray sheet-iron, to the back of the roof and looked up between the nearby high rises (modest compared with those downtown) at the TV tower and Corona Heights. The fog was gone, but the pale irregular hump of the latter still stood out sharply in the

21

morning sunlight. He looked through his binoculars, not very hopefully, but—yes, by God!—there was that crazy, drably robed worshiper, or what-not, still busy with his ritual, or whatever. If these glasses would just settle down! Now the fellow had run to a slightly lower clump of rocks and seemed to be peering furtively over it. Franz followed the apparent direction of his gaze down the crest and almost immediately came to its probable object: two hikers trudging up. Because of their colorful shorts and shirts, it was easier to make them out. Yet despite their flamboyant garb they somehow struck Franz as more respectable characters than the lurker at the summit. He wondered what would happen when they met at the top. Would the robed hierophant try to convert them? Or solemnly warn them off? Or stop them like the Ancient Mariner and tell them an eerie story with a moral? Franz looked back, but now the fellow (or could it have been a woman?) was gone. A shy type, evidently. He searched the rocks, trying to spot him hiding, and even followed the plodding hikers until they reached the top and disappeared on the other side, hoping for a surprise encounter, but none came.

Nevertheless, when he shoved the binoculars back in his pocket, he had made up his mind. He'd visit Corona Heights. It was too good a day to stay indoors.

"If you won't come to me, then I will come to you," he said aloud, quoting an eerie bit from a Montague Rhodes James ghost story and humorously applying it both to Corona Heights and to its lurker. The mountain came to Mohammed, he thought, but he had all those jinn.

6

AN HOUR AFTERWARD Franz was climbing Beaver Street, taking deep breaths to avoid panting later. He had added the bit about Time clearing her throat to *Weird Underground #7*, sealed the manuscript in its envelope, and mailed it. When he'd started, he'd had his binoculars hanging around his neck on their strap like a storybook adventurer's, so that Dorotea Luque, waiting in the lobby with a couple of elderly tenants for the mailman, had observed merrily, "You go to look for the e-scary thing to write e-stories about, no?" and he had replied. *"Sí, Señora Luque. Espectros y fantasmas,"* in what he hoped was equally cockeyed Spanish. But then a block or so back, a bit after getting off the Muni car on Market, he'd wedged them into his pocket again, alongside the street guide he'd brought. This seemed a nice enough neighborhood, quite safe-looking really; still there was no point in displaying advertisements of affluence, and Franz judged binoculars would be that even more than a camera. Too bad big cities had become—or were thought to have become—such perilous places. He'd almost chided Cal for being uptight about muggers and nuts, and look at him now. Still, he was glad he'd come alone. Exploring places he'd first studied from his window was a natural new stage in his reality trip, but a very personal one.

Actually there were relatively few people in the streets this morning. At the moment he couldn't see a single one. His mind toyed briefly with the notion of a big, modern city suddenly completely deserted, like the barque|

23

Marie Celeste or the *luxe* resort hotel in that disquietingly brilliant film *Last Year at Marienbad*.

He went by Jaime Donaldus Byers's place, a narrow-fronted piece of carpenter Gothic now painted olive with gold trim, very Old San Francisco. Perhaps he'd chance ringing the bell coming back.

From here he couldn't see Corona Heights at all. Nearby stuff masked it (and the TV tower, too). Conspicuous at a distance—he'd got a fine view of its jagged crest at Market and Duboce—it had hidden itself like a pale brown tiger on his approach, so that he had to get out his street guide and spread its map to make sure he hadn't got off the track.

Beyond Castro the way got very steep, so that he stopped twice to even out his breathing.

At last he came out on a short dead-end cross street behind some new apartments. At its other end a sedan was parked with two people sitting in the front seats—then he saw that he'd mistaken headrests for heads. They did look so like dark little tombstones!

On the other side of the cross street were no more buildings, but green and brown terraces going up to an irregular crest against blue sky. He saw he'd finally reached Corona Heights, somewhat on the far side from his apartment.

After a leisurely cigarette, he mounted steadily past some tennis courts and lawn and up a fenced and winding hillside ramp and emerged on another dead-end street—or road, rather. He felt very good, really, in the outdoors. Gazing back the way he'd come, he saw the TV tower looking enormous (and handsomer than ever) less than a mile away, yet somehow just the right size. After a moment he realized that was because it was now the same size his binoculars magnified it to from his apartment.

Strolling to the dead end of the road, he passed a long, rambling one-story brick building with generous parking space that modestly identified itself as the Josephine Randall Junior Museum. There was a panel truck with the homely label "Sidewalk Astronomer." He recalled hearing of it from Dorotea Luque's daughter Bonita as the place where children could bring pet tame squirrels and snakes and brindled Japanese rats (and bats?) when for some reason they could no longer keep them. He also realized he'd seen its low roofs from his window.

From the dead end, a short path led him to the foot of the crest, and there on the other side was all the eastern half of San Francisco and the Bay beyond and both the bridges spread out before him.

Resolutely resisting the urge to scan in detail, he set himself to mounting the ridge by the hard gravelly path near its crest. This soon became rather tiresome. He had to pause more than once for breath and set his feet carefully to keep from slipping.

When he'd about reached the spot where he'd first seen the hikers, he suddenly realized that he'd grown rather childishly apprehensive. He almost wished he had brought Gun and Saul, or run into other climbers of the solid, respectable sort, no matter how colorfully clad or otherwise loud and noisy. At the moment he wouldn't even object to a transistor radio blatting. He was pausing now not so much for breath as to scan very carefully each rock clump before circling by it, for if he thrust his head too trustingly around one, what face or no-face might he not see?

This really was too childish of him, he told himself. Didn't he want to meet the character on the summit and find out just what sort of an oddball he was? A gentle soul, most likely, from his simple garb and timidity and love of solitude. Though of course he most likely had departed by now.

Nevertheless Franz kept using his eyes systematically as he mounted the last of the slope, gentler now, to its top.

The ultimate outcropping of rocks (the Corona? the crown?) was more extensive and higher than the others. After holding back a bit (to spy out the best route, he told himself), he mounted by three ledges, each of which required a leg-stretching step, to the very top, where he at last stood up (though rather carefully, bracing his feet

wide—there was a lot of wind from the Pacific up here)
with all of Corona Heights beneath him.

He slowly turned around in a full circle, tracing the
horizon but scanning very thoroughly all the clumps of
rock and all the brown and green slopes immediately
below him, familiarizing himself with his new surroundings and incidentally ascertaining that there wasn't another being besides himself anywhere on Corona Heights.

Then he went down a couple of ledges and settled
himself comfortably in a natural rock seat facing east,
completely out of the wind. He felt very much at ease and
remarkably secure in this eyrie, especially with the sense
of the mighty TV tower rising behind him like a protective
goddess. While smoking another leisurely cigarette, he
surveyed with unaided eyes the great spread of the city
and Bay with its great ships tinier than toys, from the
faintly greenish thin pillow of smog over San Jose in the
south to the dim little pyramid of Mount Diablo beyond
Berkeley and on to the red towers of the Golden Gate
Bridge in the north with Mount Tamalpais beyond them.
It was interesting how landmarks shifted with this new
vantage point. Compared with his view from the roof,
some of the downtown buildings had shot up, while others
seemed trying to hide behind their neighbors.

After another cigarette he got out his binoculars and put
their strap around his neck and began to study this and
that. They were quite steady now, not like this morning.
He chucklingly spelled out a few big billboards south of
Market on the Embarcadero in the Mission, mostly ads for
cigarettes and beer and vodka—that Black Velvet
theme!—and a couple of the larger topless spots for the
tourists.

After a survey of the steely, gleaming inner waters and
following the Bay Bridge all the way to Oakland, he set in
seriously on the downtown buildings and soon discovered
to his embarrassment that they were quite hard to identify
from here. Distance and perspective had subtly altered
their hues and arrangement. And then contemporary skyscrapers were so very anonymous—no signs or names, no

pinnacle statues or weathercocks or crosses, no distinctive facades and cornices, no architectural ornament at all: just huge blank slabs of featureless stone, or concrete or glass that was either sleekly bright with sun or dark with shadow. Really, they might well be the "gargantuan tombs or monstrous vertical coffins of living humanity, a breeding ground for the worst of paramental entities" that old de Castries had kept ranting about in his book.

After another stretch of telescopic study in which he managed to identify a couple of the shifty skyscrapers, at last, he let his binoculars hang and got out from his other pocket the meat sandwich he'd made himself. As he unwrapped and slowly ate it, he thought of what a fortunate person he really was. A year ago he'd been a mess, but now—

He heard a *scrutch* of gravel, then another. He looked around but didn't see anything. He couldn't decide from what direction the faint sounds had come. The sandwich was dry in his mouth.

With an effort he swallowed and continued eating, and recaptured his train of thought. Yes, now he had friends like Gun and Saul . . . and Cal . . . and his health was a damn sight better, and best of all, his work was going well, his precious stories (well, precious to him) and even that terrible *Weird Underground* stuff—

Another *scrutch*, louder, and with it an odd little high-pitched laugh. He tensed himself and looked around quickly, sandwich and thoughts forgotten.

There came the laugh again, mounting toward a shrill shriek, and from behind the rocks there came dashing, along the path just below, two little girls in dark blue playclothes. The one caught the other and they spun around, squealing happily, in a whirl of sun-browned limbs and fair hair.

Franz had barely time to think what a refutation this was of Cal's (and his own) worries about this area, and for the afterthought that still it didn't seem right for parents to let such small, attractive girls (they couldn't be more than seven or eight) ramble in such a lonely place, when there came loping from behind the rocks a shaggy Saint Bernard, whom the girls at once pulled into their whirling game. But after only a little more of that, they ran on along the path by which Franz had come up, their large protector close behind. They'd either not seen Franz at all or else, after the way of little girls, they'd pretended not to notice him. He smiled at how the incident had demonstrated his unsuspected residual nervousness. His sandwich no longer tasted dry.

He crumpled the wax paper into a ball and stuck it in his pocket. The sun was already westering and striking the distant tall walls confronting him. His trip and climb had taken longer than he'd realized, and he'd been sitting here longer too. What was that epitaph Dorothy Sayers had seen on an old tombstone and thought the acme of all grue? Oh, yes: "It is later than you think." They'd made a popular song of that just before World War Two: "Enjoy yourself, enjoy yourself, it's later than you think." There was shivery irony for you. But he had lots of time.

He got busy with his binoculars again, studying the medieval greenish brown cap of the Mark Hopkins Hotel housing the restaurant-bar Top of the Mark. Grace Cathedral atop Nob Hill was masked by the high rises there, but the modernistic cylinder of St. Mary's Cathedral stood out plainly on newly named Cathedral Hill. An obviously pleasant task occurred to him: to spot his own seven-story apartment house. From his window he could see Corona Heights. Ergo, from Corona Heights he could see his window. It would be in a narrow slot between two high rises, he reminded himself, but the sun would be striking into that slot by now, giving good illumination.

To his chagrin, it proved extremely difficult. From here the lesser roofs were almost a trackless sea, literally, and such a foreshortened one that it was very hard to trace the line of streets—a checkerboard viewed from the edge. The job preoccupied him so that he became oblivious of his immediate surroundings. If the little girls had returned now and stared up at him, he probably wouldn't have noticed them. Yet the silly little problem he'd set himself was so puzzling that more than once he almost gave it up.

Really, a city's roofs were a whole dark alien world of their own, unsuspected by the myriad dwellers below, and with their own inhabitants, no doubt, their own ghosts and "paramental entities."

But he rose to the challenge and with the help of a couple of familiar watertanks he knew to be on roofs close to his and of a sign BEDFORD HOTEL painted in big black letters high on the side wall of that nearby building, he at last identified his apartment house.

He was wholly engrossed in his task.

Yes, there was the slot, by God! and there was his own window, the second from the top, very tiny but distinct in the sunlight. Lucky he'd spotted it now—the shadow traveling across the wall would soon obscure it.

And then his hands were suddenly shaking so that he'd dropped his binoculars. Only his strap kept them from crashing on the rocks.

A pale brown shape had leaned out of his window and waved at him.

What was going through his head was a couple of lines from that bit of silly folk doggerel which begins:

Taffy was a Welshman, Taffy was a thief.
Taffy came to my house and stole a piece of beef.

But it was the ending that was repeating itself in his head:

I went to Taffy's house, Taffy wasn't home.
Taffy went to my house and stole a marrowbone.

Now for God's sake don't get so excited, he told himself, taking hold of the dangling binoculars and raising them again. And stop breathing so hard—you haven't been running.

He was some time locating his building and the slot again—damn the dark sea of roofs!—but when he did, there was the shape again in his window. Pale brown, like old bones—now don't get morbid! It could be the drapes, he told himself, half blown out of his window by the wind—he'd left it open. There were freakish winds among high buildings. His drapes were green, of course, but their lining was a nondescript hue like this. And the figure wasn't waving to him now—its dancing was that of the binoculars—but rather regarding him thoughtfully as if saying, "You chose to visit my place, Mr. Westen, so I decided to make use of that opportunity to have a quiet look at yours." Quit it! he told himself. The last thing we need now is a writer's imagination.

He lowered his binoculars to give his heartbeat a chance to settle down and to work his cramped fingers. Suddenly anger filled him. In his fantasizing he'd lost sight of the plain fact that someone was mucking about in his room! But who? Dorotea Luque had a master key, of course, but she was never a bit sneaky, nor her grave brother Fernando, who did the janitor work and had hardly any English at all but played a remarkably strong game of chess. Franz had given his own duplicate key to Gun a week ago—a matter of a parcel to be delivered when he was out—and hadn't got it back. Which meant that either Gun or Saul— or Cal, for that matter—might have it now. Cal had a big old faded bathrobe she sometimes mucked around in—

But no, it was ridiculous to suspect any of them. But what about what he'd overheard from Saul on the stairs?—the 'e-stealer' Dorotea Luque had been worried about. That made more sense. Face up to it, he told himself: while he was gadding about out here, satisfying obscure aesthetic curiosities, some sneak-thief, probably on hard drugs, had somehow got into his apartment and was ripping him off.

He took up the binoculars again in a hard fury and found his apartment at once, but this time he was too late. While he'd been steadying his nerves and wildly speculating, the sun had moved on, the slot had filled with shadow, so that he could no longer make out his window, let alone any figure in it.

His anger faded. He realized it had been mostly reaction to his little shock at what he'd seen, or thought he'd seen . . . no, he'd seen something, but as to exactly what, who could be sure?

He stood up on his rocky seat, rather slowly, for his legs were a bit numb from sitting and his back was stiff, and he stepped carefully up into the wind again. He felt depressed—and no wonder, for streamers of fog were blowing in from the west, around the TV tower and half masking it; there were shadows everywhere. Corona Heights had lost its magic for him; he just wanted to get off it as soon as possible (and back to check his room), so after a quick look at his map, he headed straight down the far side, as the hikers had. Really, he couldn't get home too soon.

7

THE FAR SIDE of Corona Heights, which faced Buena Vista Park and turned its back on the central city, was steeper than it looked. Several times Franz had to restrain his impulse to hurry and make himself move carefully. Then, halfway down, a couple of big dogs came to circle and snarl at him, not Saint Bernards but those black Dobermans that always made one think of the SS. Their owner down below took his time calling them off, too. Franz almost ran across the green field at the hill's base and through the small door in the high wire fence.

He thought of phoning Mrs. Luque or even Cal, and asking them to check out his room, but hesitated to expose them to possible danger—or upset Cal while she was practicing—while as for Gun and Saul, they'd be out.

Besides, he was no longer certain what he most suspected and in any case liked to handle things alone.

Soon—but not too soon for him, by any means—he was hurrying along Buena Vista Drive East. The park it closely skirted—another elevation, but a wooded one—mounted up from beside him dark green and full of shadows. In his present mood it looked anything but a "good view" to him, rather an ideal spot for heroin intrigues and sordid murders. The sun was altogether gone by now, and ragged arms of fog came curving after him. When he got to Duboce, he wanted to rush down, but the sidewalks were too steep—as steep as any he'd seen on any of San Francisco's more than seven hills—and once again he had to grit his teeth and place his feet with care and take his time. The neighborhood seemed quite as

safe as Beaver Street, but there were few people out in the
chilly change of weather, and once more he stuffed his
binoculars back into his pocket.

He caught the N-Judah car where it comes out of the
tunnel under Buena Vista Park (Frisco's hills were hon-
eycombed with 'em, he thought) and rode it down Market
to the Civic Center. Among the crowders boarding a 19-
Polk there, a hulking drab shape lurching up behind him
gave him a start, but it was only a blank-eyed workman
powdered with pale dust from some demolition job.

He got off the 19 at Geary. In the lobby of 811 Geary
there was only Fernando vacuuming, a sound as gray and
hollow as the day had grown outside. He would have liked
to chat, but the short man, blocky and somber as a Peruvian idol, had less English than his sister and was additionally rather deaf. They bowed gravely to each other,
exchanged a "Senyor Loókay" and a "meestair Juestón," Fernando's rendering of "Westen."

He rode the creaking elevator up to six. He had the
impulse to stop at Cal's or the boys' first, but it was a
matter of—well, courage—not to. The hall was dark (a
ceiling globe was out) and the shaft-window and knobless
closet door next to his room darker. As he approached his
own door, he realized his heart was thumping. Feeling
both foolish and apprehensive, he slipped his key into the
lock, and clutching his binoculars in his other hand as an
impromptu weapon, he thrust the door swiftly open and
quickly switched on the ceiling light inside.

The 200-watt glare showed his room empty and undisturbed. From the inside of the still-tousled bed, his colorful "scholar's mistress" seemed to wink at him humorously. Nevertheless, he didn't feel secure until he'd rather
shamefacedly peered in the bathroom and then opened the
closet and the tall clothes cabinet and glanced inside.

He switched off the top light then and went to the open
window. The green drapes were lined with a sun-faded
tan, all right, but if they'd been blown halfway out the
window at some point, a chance of wind had blown them
neatly back into place afterward. The serrated hump of

Corona Heights showed up dimly through the advancing
high fog. The TV tower was wholly veiled. He looked
down and saw that the windowsill and his narrow desk
abutting it and the carpet at his feet were all strewn with
crumbles of brownish paper that reminded him of Gun's
paper-shredding machine. He recalled that he'd been
handling some old pulp magazines here yesterday, tearing
out pages he wanted to save. Had he thrown the
magazines away afterward? He couldn't remember, but
probably—they weren't lying around anywhere nearby,
at any rate, only a neat little stack of ones he hadn't looted
yet. Well, a thief who stole only gutted old pulp
magazines was hardly a serious menace—more like a
trashman, a helpful scavenger.

The tension that had been knotting him departed at last.
He realized he was very thirsty. He got a split of ginger ale
from the small refrigerator and drank it eagerly. While he
made coffee on the hot plate, he sketchily straightened the
disordered half of the bed and turned on the shaded light at
its head. He carried over his coffee and the two books he'd
shown Cal that morning, and settled himself comfortably,
and read around in them and speculated.

When he realized it was getting darker outside, he
poured himself more coffee and carried it down to Cal's.
The door was ajar. Inside, Cal's shoulders were lifting
rhythmically as she played with furious precision, her ears
covered with large padded phones. Franz couldn't be sure
whether he heard the ghost of a concerto, or only the very
faint thuds of the keys.

Saul and Gun were talking quietly on the couch, Gun
with a green bottle beside him. Remembering this morning's bitter words he'd overheard, Franz looked for signs
of strain, but all seemed harmony. Perhaps he'd read too
much into their words.

Saul Rosenzweig, a thin man with dark hair shoulder-
length and dark-circled eyes, quirked a smile and said,
"Hello, Calvina asked us down to keep her company
while she practices, though you'd think a couple of window dummies could do the job as well. But Calvina's a

romantic puritan at heart. Deep inside she wants to frustrate us."

Cal had taken off her headphones and stood up. Without a word or a look at anyone, or anything apparently, she picked up some clothes and vanished like a sleepwalker into the bathroom, whence there came presently the sound of showering.

Gun grinned at Franz and said, "Greetings. Sit down and join the devotees of silence. How goes the writer's life?"

They talked inconsequentially and lazily of this and that. Saul carefully made a long thin cigarette. Its piney smoke was pleasant, but Franz and Gun smilingly declined to share, Gun tilting his green bottle for a long swallow.

Cal reappeared in a surprisingly short time, looking fresh and demure in a dark brown dress. She poured herself a tall thin glass of orange juice from the fridge and sat down.

"Saul," she said quietly, "you know my long name is not Calvina, but Calpurnia—the minor Roman Cassandra who kept warning Caesar. I may be a puritan, but I wasn't named for Calvin. My parents were both born Presbyterians, it's true, but my father early progressed into Unitarianism and died a devout Ethical Culturist. He used to pray to Emerson and swear by Robert Ingersoll. While my mother was, rather frivolously, into Bahai. And I don't own a couple of window dummies, or I might use them. No, no pot, thank you. I have to hold myself intact until tomorrow night. Gun, thanks for humoring me. It does help to have people in the room, even when I'm incommunicada. It helps especially when evening begins to close in. That ale smells wonderful, but alas . . . same reason as no pot. Franz, you're looking quietly prodigious. What happened at Corona Heights?"

Pleased that she had been thinking about him and observing him so closely and accurately, Franz told the story of his adventure. He was struck by how in the telling it became rather trivial-seeming and less frightening, though paradoxically more entertaining—the writer's curse and blessing.

Gun happily summed up. "So you go to investigate this apparition or what-not, and find it's pulled the big switch and is thumbing its nose at you from your own window two miles away. 'Taffy went to my house'—that's neat."

Saul said, "Your Taffy story reminds me of my Mr. Edwards. He gets the idea that two enemies in a parked car across the street from the hospital have got a pain-ray projector trained on him. We wheel him over there so he can see for himself there ain't no one in any of the cars. He's very much relieved and keeps thanking us, but when we get him back to his room, he lets out a sudden squeal of agony. Seems his enemies have taken advantage of his absence to plant a pain-ray projector somewhere in the walls."

"Oh, Saul," Cal said in mildly scathing tones, "we're not all of us your hospital people—at least yet. Franz, I wonder if those two innocent-seeming little girls may not have been involved. You said they were running around and dancing, like your pale brown thing. I'm sure that if there's such a thing as psychic energy, little girls have lots of it."

"I'd say you have a good artistic imagination. That angle hadn't even occurred to me," Franz told her, acutely aware that he was beginning to disparage the whole incident, but unable to help himself. "Saul, I may very well have been projecting—at least in part—but if so, what? Also, the figure was nondescript, remember, and wasn't doing anything objectively sinister."

Saul said, "Look, I wasn't suggesting any parallel. That's your idea, and Cal's. I was just reminded of another weird incident."

Gun guffawed. "Saul doesn't think we're all completely crazy. Just fringe-psychotic."

There was a knock and then the door opened as Dorotea Luque let herself in. She sniffed and looked at Saul. She was a slender version of her brother, with a beautiful Inca profile and jet-black hair. She had a small parcel-post package of books for Franz.

"I wondered you'd be down here, and then I heard you talk," she explained. "Did you find the e-scary things to write about with your . . . how you say. . . ?" She made binoculars of her hands and held them to her eyes, and then looked questioningly around when they all laughed.

While Cal got her a glass of wine, Franz hastened to explain. To his surprise, she took the figure in the window very seriously.

"But are you e-sure you weren't ripped off?" she demanded anxiously. "We had an e-stealer on the second floor, I think."

"My portable TV and tape recorder were there," he told her. "A thief would take those first."

"But how about your marrowbone?" Saul put in. "Taffy get that?"

"And did you close your transom and double-lock your door?" Dorotea persisted, illustrating with a vigorous twist of her wrist. "Is double-lock now?"

"I always double-lock it," Franz assured her. "I used to think it was only in detective stories they slipped locks with a plastic card. But then I found I could slip my own with a photograph. The transom, no. I like it open for ventilation."

"Should always close the transom, too, when you go out," she pronounced. "All of you, you hear me? Is thin people can get through transoms, you better believe. Well, I am glad you weren't ripped off. *Gracias*," she added, nodding to Cal as she sipped her wine.

Cal smiled and said to Saul and Gun, "Why shouldn't a modern city have its special ghosts, like castles and graveyards and big old manor houses once had?"

Saul said, "My Mrs. Willis thinks the skyscrapers are out to get her. At night they make themselves still skinnier, she says, and come sneaking down the streets after her."

Gun said, "I once heard lightning whistle over

Chicago. There was a thunderstorm over the Loop, and I
was on the South Side at the university, right near the site
of the first atomic pile. There'd be a flash on the northern
horizon and then, seven seconds later, not thunder, but
this high-pitched moaning scream. I had the idea that all
the elevated tracks were audio-resonating a radio compo-
nent of the flash.''

Cal said eagerly, "Why mightn't the sheer mass of all
that steel—? Franz, tell them about the book.''

He repeated what he'd told her this morning about
Megapolisomancy and a little besides.

Gun broke in. "And he says our modern cities are our
Egyptian pyramids? That's beautiful. Just imagine how,
when we've all been killed off by pollution (nuclear,
chemical, smothered in unbiodegradable plastic, red tides
of dying microlife, the nasty climax of our climax culture), an archaeological expedition arrives by spaceship
from another solar system and starts to explore us like a
bunch of goddam Egyptologists! They'd use roving robot
probes to spy through our utterly empty cities, which
would be too dangerously radioactive for anything else, as
dead and deadly as our poisoned seas. What would they
make of the World Trade Center in New York City and
the Empire State Building? Or the Sears Building in
Chicago? Or even the Transamerica Pyramid here? Or
that space-launch assembly building at Canaveral that's
so big you can fly light planes around inside? They'd
probably decide they were all built for religious and occult
purposes, like Stonehenge. They'd never imagine people
lived and worked there. No question, our cities will be the
eeriest ruins ever. Franz, this de Castries had a sound
idea—the sheer amount of stuff there is in cities. That's
heavy, heavy.''

Saul put in, "Mrs. Willis says the skyscrapers get very
heavy at night when they—excuse me—screw her.''

Dorotea Luque's eyes grew large, then she exploded in
giggles. "Oh, that's naughty,'' she reproved him merrily,
wagging a finger. .

Saul's eyes got a faraway look like a mad poet's, and he

embroidered his remark with, ''Can't you imagine their tall gray skinny forms sneaking sideways down the streets, one flying buttress erected for a stony phallus?'' and there was more sputtery laughter from Mrs. Luque. Gun got her more wine and himself another bottle of ale.

8

CAL SAID, "Franz, I've been thinking on and off all day, in the corner of my mind that wasn't Brandenburging, about that '607 Rhodes' that drew you to move here. Was it a definite place? And if so, where?"

"607 Rhodes—what's that all about?" Saul asked.

Franz explained again about the rice-paper journal and the violet-ink person who might have been Clark Ashton Smith and his possible interviews with de Castries. Then he said, "The 607 can't be a street address—like 811 Geary here, say. There's no such street as Rhodes in 'Frisco. I've checked. The nearest to it is a Rhode Island Street, but that's way over in the Potrero, and it's clear from the entries that the 607 place is here downtown, within easy walking distance of Union Square. And once the journal-keeper describes looking out the window at Corona Heights and Mount Sutro—of course, there wasn't any TV tower then—"

"Hell, in 1928 there weren't even the Bay and Golden Gate Bridges," Gun put in.

"—and at Twin Peaks," Franz went on. "And then he says that Thibaut always referred to Twin Peaks as Cleopatra's Breasts."

"I wonder if skyscrapers ever have breasts," Saul said. "I must ask Mrs. Willis about that."

Dorotea bugged her eyes again, indicated her bosom, said, "Oh, no!" and once more burst into laughter.

Cal said, "Maybe Rhodes is the name of a building or hotel. You know, the Rhodes Building."

"Not unless the name's been changed since 1928,"

Franz told her. "There's nothing like that now that I've heard of. The name Rhodes strike a bell with any of you?"

It didn't.

Gun speculated, "I wonder if *this* building ever had a name, the poor old raddled dear."

"You know," Cal said, "I'd like to know that too."

Dorotea shook her head. "Is just 811 Geary. Was once hotel maybe—you know, night clerk and maids. But I don't know."

"Buildings Anonymous," Saul remarked without looking up from the reefer he was making.

"Now we do close transom," said Dorotea, suiting actions to words. "Okay smoke pot. But do not—how you say?—advertise."

Heads nodded wisely.

After a bit they all decided that they were hungry and should eat together at the German Cook's around the corner because it was his night for sauerbraten. Dorotea was persuaded to join them. On the way she picked up her daughter Bonita and the taciturn Fernando, who now beamed.

Walking together behind the others, Cal asked Franz, "Taffy is something more serious than you're making out, isn't it?"

He had to agree, though he was becoming curiously uncertain of some of the things that had happened today— the usual not-unpleasant evening fog settling around his mind like a ghost of the old alcoholic one. High in the sky, the lopsided circle of the gibbous moon challenged the street lights.

He said, "When I thought I saw that thing in my window, I strained for all sorts of explanations, to avoid having to accept a . . . well, supernatural one. I even thought it might have been you in your old bathrobe."

"Well, it could have been me, except it wasn't," she said calmly. "I've still got your key, you know. Gun gave it to me that day your big package was coming and Dorotea was out. I'll give it to you after dinner."

"No hurry," he said.

"I wish we could figure out that 607 Rhodes," she said, "and the name of our own building, if it ever had one."

"I'll try to think of a way," he said. "Cal, did your father actually swear by Robert Ingersoll?"

"Oh, yes—'In the name of . . .' and so on—and by William James, too, and Felix Adler, the man who founded Ethical Culture. His rather atheistic coreligionists thought it odd of him, but he liked the ring of sacerdotal language. He thought of science as a sacrament."

Inside the friendly little restaurant, Gun and Saul were shoving two tables together with the smiling approval of blonde and red-cheeked Rose, the waitress. The way they ended up, Saul sat between Dorotea and Bonita with Gun on Bonita's other side. Bonita had her mother's black hair, but was already a half-head taller and otherwise looked quite Anglo—the narrow-bodied and -faced North European type; nor was there any trace of Spanish in her American schoolgirl voice. He recalled hearing that her divorced and now nameless father had been black Irish. Though pleasingly slim in sweater and slacks, she looked somewhat gawky—very far from the shadowy, hurrying shape that had briefly excited him this morning and awakened an unpleasant memory.

He sat beside Gun with Cal between himself and Fernando, who was next to his sister. Rose took their orders.

Gun switched to a dark beer. Saul ordered a bottle of red wine for himself and the Luques. The sauerbraten was delicious, the potato pancakes with applesauce out of this world. Bela, the gleaming-faced German Cook (Hungarian, actually) had outdone himself.

In a lull in the conversation, Gun said to Franz, "That was really a very strange thing that happened to you on Corona Heights. As near as you can get today to what you'd call the supernatural."

Saul heard and said at once, "Hey, what's a materialist scientist like you doing talking about the supernatural?"

"Come off it, Saul," Gun answered with a chuckle. "I

deal with matter, sure. But what is that? Invisible parti-
cles, waves, and force fields. Nothing solid at all. Don't
teach your grandmother to suck eggs.''

"You're right," Saul grinned, sucking his. "There's
no reality but the individual's immediate sensations, his
awareness. All else is inference. Even the individuals are
inference.''

Cal said, "I think the only reality is number . . . and
music, which comes to the same thing. They are both real
and they both have power.''

"My computers agree with you, all the way down the
line," Gun told her. "Number is all they know. Music?—
well, they could learn that.''

Franz said, "I'm glad to hear you all talk that way. You
see, supernatural horror is my bread and butter, both that
Weird Underground trash—''

Bonita protested,''No!''

"—and the more serious junk, but sometimes people
tell me there's no such thing as supernatural horror any-
more—that science has solved, or can solve, all mysteries, that religion is just another name for social service,
and that modern people are too sophisticated and knowl-
edgeable to be scared of ghosts even for kicks.''

"Don't make me laugh," Gun said. "Science has only
increased the area of the unknown. And if there is a god,
her name is Mystery.''

Saul said, "Refer those brave erudite skeptics to my
Mr. Edwards or Mrs. Willis, or simply to their own
inevitable buried fears. Or refer 'em to me, and I'll tell
'em the story of the Invisible Nurse who terrorized the
locked ward at St. Luke's. And then there was . . ." He
hesitated, glancing toward Cal. "No, that's too long a
story to tell now.''

Bonita looked disappointed. Her mother said eagerly,
"But are e-strange things. In Lima. This city too. *Bru-
jas*—how you say?—witches!'' She shuddered happily.

Her brother beamed his understanding and lifted a hand
to preface one of his rare remarks. "*Hay hechiceria*," he
said vehemently, with a great air of making himself clear,

"*Hechiceria ocultado en murallas*." He crouched a little, looking up. "*Murallas muy altas*."

Everyone nodded pleasantly as if they understood.

Franz asked Cal in a low voice, "What's that *hechi*?"

She whispered, "Witchcraft, I think. Witchcraft hidden in the walls. Very high walls." She shrugged.

Franz murmured, "Where in the walls, I wonder? Like Mr. Edward's pain-ray projector?"

Gun said, "There's one thing, though, Franz, I do wonder about—whether you really identified your own window correctly from Corona. You said the roofs were like a sea on edge. It reminds me of difficulties I've run into in identifying localities in photographs of stars, or pictures of the earth taken from satellites. The sort of trouble every amateur astronomer runs into—the pros, too. So many times you come across two or more localities that are almost identical."

"I've thought of that myself," Franz said. "I'll check it out."

Leaning back, Saul said, "Say, here's a good idea, let's all of us some day soon go for a picnic to Corona Heights. You and I, Gun, could bring our ladies—they'd like it. How does that grab you, Bonny?"

"Oh, yes," Bonita replied eagerly.

On that note they broke up.

Dorotea said, "We thank you for the wine. But remember, double-lock doors and close transoms when go out."

Cal said, "Now with any luck I'll sleep twelve hours. Franz, I'll give you your key some other time." Saul glanced at her.

Franz smiled and asked Fernando if he cared to play chess later that evening. The Peruvian smiled agreeably.

Bela Szlawik, sweating from his labors, himself made change as they paid their checks, while Rose fluttered about and held the door for them.

As they collected on the sidewalk outside, Saul looked toward Franz and Cal and said, "How about drifting back with Gun to my room before you play chess? I'd sort of like to tell you that story."

Franz nodded. Cal said, "Not me. Straight off to bed."
Saul nodded that he understood her.

Bonita had heard. "You're going to tell him the story of
the Invisible Nurse," she said accusingly. "I want to hear
that, too."

"No, it is time for bed," her mother asserted, not too
commandingly or confidently. "See, Cal goes bed."

"I don't care," Bonita said, pushing up against Saul
closely, invading his space. "Please? Please?" she
coaxed insistently.

Saul grabbed her suddenly, hugged her tight, and blew
down her neck with a great raspberry sound. She squealed
loudly and happily. Franz, glancing almost automatically
toward Gun, saw him start to wince, then control it, but
his lips were thin. Dorotea smiled almost as happily as if it
were her own neck being blown down. Fernando frowned
slightly and held himself with a somewhat military
dignity.

As suddenly Saul held the girl away from him and said
to her matter-of-factly, "Now look here, Bonny, this is
another story I want to tell Franz—a very dull one of
interest only to writers. There is no Story of the Invisible
Nurse. I just made that up because I needed something to
illustrate my point."

"I don't believe you," Bonita said, looking him
straight in the eye.

"Okay, you're right," he said abruptly, dropping his
hands away from her and standing back. "There *is* a Story
of the Invisible Nurse Who Terrorized the Locked Ward at
St. Luke's, and the reason I didn't tell it was not that it's
too long—it's quite short—but simply too horrible. But
now you've brought it down upon yourself and all these
other good people. So gather round, all of you."

As he stood in the dark street with the light of the
gibbous moon shining on his flashing eyes, sallow face,
and elf-locked, long dark hair, he looked very much like a
gypsy, Franz thought.

"Her name was Wortly," Saul began, dropping his
voice. "Olga Wortly, R.N.—(Registered Nurse). That's

not her real name—this became a police case and they're still looking for her—but it has the flavor of the real one. Well, Olga Wortly, R.N., was in charge of the swing shift (the four to midnight) in the locked ward at St. Luke's. And there was no terror then. In fact, she ran what was in a way the happiest and certainly the quietest swing shift ever, because she was very generous with her sleeping potions, so that the graveyard shift never had any trouble with wakeful patients and the day shift sometimes had difficulty getting some of them waked up for lunch, let alone breakfast.

"She didn't trust her L.V.N. (Licensed Vocational Nurse) to dispense her goodies. And she favored mixtures, whenever she could shade or stretch the doctor's order to allow them, because she thought two drugs were always surer than one—Librium *with* the Thorazine (she doted on Tuinal because it's *two* barbiturates: red Seconal with blue Amytal), chloral hydrate *with* the phenobarbital, paraldehyde *with* the yellow Nembutal—in fact, you could always tell when she was coming (our fairy snooze mother, our dark goddess of slumber) because the paralyzing stench of the paraldehyde always preceded her; she always managed to have at least one patient on paraldehyde. It's a superaromatic, superalcohol, you know, that tickles the top of your sinuses, and it smells like God-knows-what—super banana oil; some nurses call it gasoline—and you give it with fruit juice for a chaser and you dispense it in a glass shot-glass because it'll melt a plastic one, and its molecules travel through the air ahead of it faster than light!"

Saul had his audience well in hand, Franz noted. Dorotea was listening with as rapt delight as Bonita; Cal and Gun were smiling indulgently; even Fernando had caught the spirit and was grinning at the long drug names. For the moment the sidewalk in front of the German Cook's was a moonlit gypsy encampment, lacking only the dancing flames of an open fire.

"Every night, two hours after supper, Olga would make her druggy-wug rounds. Sometimes she'd have the

L.V.N. or an aide carry the tray, sometimes she'd carry it herself.

" 'Sleepy-bye time, Mrs. Binks,' she'd say. 'Here's your pass to dreamland. That's a good little girl. And now this lovely yellow one. Good evening, Miss Cheeseley, I've got your trip to Hawaii for you—blue for the deep blue ocean, red for the sunset skies. And now a sip of the bitter to wash it down—think of the dark salt waves. Hold out your tongue, Mr. Finelli, I've something to make you wise. Whoever'd think, Mr. Wong, they could put nine hours and maybe ten of good, good darkness into such a tiny time-capsule, a gelatin spaceship bound for the stars. You smelled us coming, didn't you, Mr. Auerbach? Grape juice chaser tonight!' And so on and so on.

"And so Olga Wortly, R.N., our mistress of oblivion, our queen of dreams, kept the locked ward happy," Saul continued, "and even won high praise—for everyone likes a quiet ward—until one night she went just a little too far and the next morning every last patient had O.D.'ed (overdosed) and was D.O.A. (that's Dead on Arrival, Bonny) with a beatific smile on his or her face. And Olga Wortly was gone, never to be seen again.

"Somehow they managed to hush it up—I think they blamed it on an epidemic of galloping hepatitis or malignant eczema—and they're still looking for Olga Wortly."

"That's about all there is to it," he said with a shrug, relaxing, "except"—he held up a finger dramatically, and his voice went low and eerie—"except they say that on nights when there's a lot of moonlight, just like this now, and it's sleepy-bye time, and the L.V.N. is about to start out with her tray of night medicines in their cute little paper favor cups, you get a whiff of paraldehyde at the nurses' station (although they *never* use that drug there now) and it travels from room to room and from bed to bed, not missing one, that unmistakable whiff does—the Invisible Nurse making her rounds!"

And with more or less appropriate oohs, ahs, and chuckles, they set out for home in a body. Bonita seemed satisfied. Dorotea said extravagantly, "Oh, I am frightened! When I wake up tonight, I think nurse coming I can't see make me swallow that parry-alley stuff."

"Par-al-de-hyde," Fernando said slowly, but with surprising accuracy.

9

THERE WAS SO much stuff in Saul's room and such a variety of it, apparently unorganized (in this respect it was the antithesis of Gun's), that you wondered why it wasn't a mess—until you realized that nothing in it looked thrown away or tossed aside, everything looked loved: the stark and unglamorized photographs of people, mostly elderly (they turned out to be patients at the hospital, Saul pointed out Mr. Edwards and Mrs. Willis); books from Merck's Manual to Colette, *The Family of Man* to Henry Miller, Edgar Rice to Wiliiam S. Burroughs to George Borrow (*The Gypsies in Spain*, *Wild Wales*, and *The Zincali*); a copy of Nostig's *The Subliminal Occult* (that really startled Franz); a lot of hippie, Indian, and American Indian beadwork; hash-smoking accessories; a beer stein filled with fresh flowers; an eye chart; a map of Asia; and a number of paintings and drawings from childish to mathematical to wild, including a striking acrylic abstraction on black cardboard that teemed with squirming shapes and jewel and insect colors and seemed to reproduce in miniature the room's beloved confusion.

Saul indicated it, saying, "I did that the one time I took cocaine. If there is a drug (which I doubt) that adds something to the mind instead of just taking away, then it's cocaine. If I ever went the drug route again, that'd be my choice."

"Again?" Gun asked quizzically, indicating the pot paraphernalia.

"Pot is a plaything," Saul averred, "a frivolity, a social lubricant to be classed with tobacoo, coffee, and the

49

other tea. When Anslinger got Congress to classify it as—
for all practical purposes—a hard drug, he really loused
up the development of American society and the mobility
of its classes.''

"As much as that?'' Gun began skeptically.

"It's certainly not in the same league as alcohol,''
Franz agreed, "which mostly has the community's blessing, at least the advertising half of it: Drink booze and you
will be sexy, healthy, and wealthy, the ads say, especially
those Black Velvet ones. You know, Saul, it was funny
you should bring paraldehyde into your story. The last
time I was 'separated' from alcohol—to use that oh-so-
delicate medical expression—I got a little paraldehyde for
three nights running. It really was delightful—the same
effect as alcohol when I first drank it—a sensation I
thought I'd never experience again, that warm, rosy
glow.''

Saul nodded. "It does the same job as alcohol, without
so much immediate wear and tear on the chemical systems. So the person who's worn out with drinking ordinary booze responds to it nicely. But of course it can
become addictive, too, as I'm sure you know. Say, how
about more coffee? I've only got the freeze-dried, of
course.''

As he quickly set water to boil and measured brown
crystals into colorful mugs, Gun ventured, "But wouldn't
you say that alcohol is mankind's natural drug, with
thousands of years of use and expertise behind it—learning its ways, becoming seasoned to it.''

"Time enough, at any rate,'' Saul commented, "for it
to kill off all the Italians, Greeks, Jews, and other
Mediterraneans with an extreme genetic weakness in respect to it. The American Indians and Eskimos aren't so
lucky. They're still going through that. But hemp and
peyote and the poppy and the mushroom have pretty long
histories, too.''

"Yes, but there you get into the psychedelic, con-
sciousness-distorting (I'd say, instead of -enlarging) sort

of thing," Gun protested, "while alcohol has a more straightforward effect."

"I've had hallucinations from alcohol, too," Franz volunteered in partial contradiction, "though not so extreme as those you get from acid, from what they tell me. But only during withdrawal, oddly, the first three days. In closets and dark corners and under tables—never in very bright light—I'd see these black and sometimes red wires, about the thickness of telephone cords, vibrating, whipping around. Made me think of giant spiders' legs and such. I'd know they were hallucinations—they were manageable, thank God. Bright light would always wipe them out."

"Withdrawal's a funny and sometimes touch-and-go business," Saul observed as he poured boiling water. "That's when drinkers get delirium tremens, not when they're drinking—I'm sure you know that, too. But the perils and agonies of withdrawal from the hard drugs have been vastly exaggerated—it's part of the mythos. I learned that when I was a paramedical worker in the great days of the Haight-Ashbury, before I became a nurse, running around and giving Thorazine to hippies who'd O.D.'d or thought they had."

"Is that true?" Franz asked, accepting his coffee. "I've always heard that quitting heroin cold turkey was about the worst."

"Part of the mythos," Saul assured Franz, shaking his long-haired head as he handed Gun his coffee and began to sip his own. "The mythos that Anslinger did so much to create back in the thirties (when all the boys who'd been big in Prohibition enforcement were trying to build themselves equal narcotics jobs) when he went to Washington with a couple of veterinary doctors who knew about doping race horses and a satchel of sensational Mexican and Central American newspaper clippings about murders and rapes and such committed by peons supposedly crazed with marijuana."

"A lot of writers jumped on that bandwagon," Franz

put in. "The hero would take one drag of a strange cigarette and instantly start having weird hallucinations, mostly along the lines of sex and bloodshed. Say, maybe I could suggest a 'Weird Underground' episode bringing in the Narcotics Bureau," he added thoughtfully, more to himself than them. "It's a thought."

"And the agonies of cold-turkey withdrawal were part of that mythos picture," Saul took up, "so that when the beats and hippies and such began taking drugs as a gesture of rebellion against the establishment and their parents' generation, they started having all the dreadful hallucinations and withdrawal agonies the cop-invented mythos told them they would." He smiled crookedly. "You know, I've sometimes thought it was very similar to the long-range effects of war propaganda on the Germans. In World War Two they committed all the atrocities, and more, that they were accused of, mostly falsely, in World War One. I hate to say it, but people are always trying to live up to worst expectations."

Gun added, "The hippie-era analogue to the SS Nazis being the Manson Family."

"At any rate," Saul resumed, "that's what I learned when I was rushing around the Hashbury at dead of night, giving Thorazine to flipping flower children *per anum*. I couldn't use a hypodermic needle because I wasn't a real nurse yet."

Gun put in reflectively, "That's how Saul and I met."

"But it wasn't to Gun I was giving the rectal Thorazine," Saul amended. "—that would have been just too romantic—but to a friend of his, who'd O.D.'ed, then called him up, so he called us. That's how we met."

"My friend recovered very nicely," Gun put in.

"How did you both meet Cal?" Franz asked.

"When she moved here," Gun said.

"At first it was only as if a silence had descended on us," Saul said thoughtfully. "For the previous occupant of her room had been exceptionally noisy, even for this building."

Gun said, "And then it was as if a very quiet but

musical mouse had joined the population. Because we became aware of hearing flute music, we thought it was, but so soft we couldn't be sure we weren't imagining it.''

"At the same time," Saul said, "we began to notice this attractive, uncommunicative, very polite young woman who'd get on or off at four, always alone and always opening and closing the elevator gates very gently.''

Gun said, "And then one evening we went to hear some Beethoven quartets at the Veterans Building. She was in the audience and we introduced ourselves.''

"All three of us taking the initiative," Saul added. "By the end of the concert we were pals.''

"And the next weekend we were helping her redecorate her apartment," Gun finished. "It was as if we'd known each other for years.''

"Or at least as if she'd known us for years," Saul qualified. "We were a lot longer learning about her—what an incredibly overprotected life she'd led, her difficulties with her mother . . .''

"How hard her father's death hit her . . .'' Gun threw in.

"And how determined she was to make a go of things on her own and"—Saul shrugged—"and learn about life.'' He looked at Franz. "We were even longer discovering just how sensitive she was under that cool and competent exterior of hers,and also about her abilities in addition to the musical.''

Franz nodded, then asked Saul, "And now are you going to tell me the story about her you've been saving?''

"How did you know it was going to be about her?'' the other inquired.

"Because you glanced at her before you decided not to tell it at the restaurant," Franz told him, "and because you didn't really invite me over until you were sure she wouldn't be coming.''

"You writers are pretty sharp," Saul observed. "Well, this happens to be a writer's story, in a way. Your sort of writer—the supernatural horror sort. Your Corona Heights thing made me want to tell it. The same realm of the unknown, but a different country in it.''

Franz wanted to say, ''I had rather anticipated that, too,'' but he refrained.

10

SAUL LIT A cigarette and settled himself back against the wall. Gun occupied the other end of the couch. Franz was in the armchair facing them.

"Early on," Saul began, "I realized that Cal was very interested in my people at the hospital. Not that she'd ask questions, but from the way she'd hold still whenever I mentioned them. They were one more thing in the tremendous outside world she was starting to explore that she felt compelled to learn about and sympathize with or steel herself against—with her it seems to be a combination of the two.

"Well, in those days I was pretty interested in my people myself. I'd been on the evening shift for a year and pretty well in charge of it for a couple of months, and so I had a lot of ideas about changes I wanted to make and was making. One thing, the nurse who'd been running the ward ahead of me had been overdoing the sedation, I felt." He grinned. "You see, that story I told for Bonny and Dora tonight wasn't all invented. Anyway, I'd been cutting most of them down to the point where I could communicate and work with them and they weren't still comatose at breakfast time. Of course, it makes for a livelier and sometimes more troublesome ward, but I was fresh and feisty and up to handling that."

He chuckled. "I suppose that's something almost every new person in charge does at first: cuts down on the barbiturates—until he or she gets tired and maybe a bit frazzled and decides that peace is worth a little sedation.

"But I was getting to know my people pretty well, or

55

thought I was, what stage of their cycles each was in, and so be able to anticipate their antics and keep the ward in hand. There was this young Mr. Sloan, for instance, who had epilepsy—the *petit mal* kind—along with extreme depression. He was well educated, had showed artistic talent. As he'd approach the climax of his cycle, he'd begin to have his *petit mal* attacks—you know, brief loss of consciousness, being 'not there' for a few seconds, he'd sway a little—closer and closer together, every twenty minutes or so, then even closer. You know, I've often thought that epilepsy is very much like the brain trying to give itself electroshock. At any rate, my young Mr. Sloan would climax with a seizure approximating or mimicking *grand mal* in which he'd fall to the floor and writhe and make a great racket and perform automatic acts and lose control of all his bodily functions—psychic epilepsy, they used to call it. Then his *petit mal* attacks would space themselves way out and he'd be better for a week, about. He seemed to time all this very exactly and put a lot of creative effort into it—I told you he had artistic talent. You know, all insanity is a form of artistic expression, I often think. Only the person has nothing but himself to work with—he can't get at outside materials to manipulate them—so he puts all his art into his behavior.

"Well, as I've said, I knew that Cal was getting very curious about my people, she'd even been hinting that she'd like to see them, so one night when everything was going very smoothly—all my people at a quiet stage in their cycles—I had her come over. Of course by now I was bending the hospital rules quite a bit, as you'd expect. There wasn't any moon either that night—new moon or near it—moonlight does excite people, especially the crazies—I don't know how, but it does."

"Hey, you never told me about this before," Gun interjected. "I mean, about having Cal at the hospital."

"So?" Saul said and shrugged. "Well, she arrived about an hour after the day shift left, looking somewhat pale and apprehensive but excited . . . and almost immediately everything in the ward started to get out of hand

and go wacko. Mrs. Willis began to whine and wail about her terrible misfortunes—she wasn't due to do that for a week, I'd figured, it's really heartrending to hear—and that set off Miss Craig, who's good at screaming. Mr. Schmidt, who'd been very well behaved for over a month, managed to get his pants down and unload a pile of shit before we could stop him in front of Mr. Bugatti's door, who's his 'enemy' from time to time—and we hadn't had *that* sort of thing happening on the ward since the previous year. Meanwhile, Mrs. Gutmayer had overturned her dinner tray and was vomiting, and Mr. Stowacki had somehow managed to break a plate and cut himself—and Mrs. Harper was screaming at the sight of blood (there wasn't much) and that made two of them (two screamers—not in Fay Wray's class, but good).

"Well, naturally I had to abandon Cal to her own devices while we dealt with all this, though of course I was wondering what she must be thinking and kicking myself for having invited her over at all and for being such a megalomaniac about my ability to predict and forestall disasters.

"By the time I got back to her, Cal had gone or retreated to the recreation room with young Mr. Sloan and a couple of others, and she'd discovered our piano and was quietly trying it out—horribly out of tune, of course, it must have been, at least to her ears.

"She listened to the hurried rundown I gave her on things—excuses, I suppose—we didn't usually have shit out in the halls, etcetera—and from time to time she'd nod, but she kept on working steadily at the piano at the same time, as if she were hunting for the keys that were least discordant (afterward she confirmed that that was exactly what she had been doing). She was paying attention to me, all right, but she was doing this piano thing, too.

"About then I became aware that the excitement was building up behind me in the ward again and that Harry's (young Sloan's) *petit mal* seizures were coming much closer together than they ought to, while he was pacing restlessly in a circle around the recreation room. By my count he wasn't due to climax until the next night, but now he'd unaccountably speeded up his cycle so he'd throw his *grand mal* fit tonight for sure—in a very short time, in fact.

"I started to warn Cal about what was likely to happen, but just then she sat back and screwed up her face a little, like she sometimes does when she's starting a concert, and then she began to play something very catchy of Mozart's—Cherubino's Song from *The Marriage of Figaro*, it turned out to be—but in what seemed to be the most discordant key of all on that banged-up old upright (afterward she confirmed this, too).

"Next thing, she was modulating the music into another key that was only a shade less discordant than the first, and so on and so on. Believe it or not, in her fooling around she'd worked out a succession of the keys from the most to the least discordant on that old out-of-tune loonies' piano, and now she was playing that Mozart air in all of them in the same order, least to most harmonious— Cherubino's Song, the words to which go something like (in English) 'We who love's power surely do feel—why should it ever through my heart steal?' And then there's something about 'in my sorrow lingers delight.'

"Meanwhile, I could feel the tensions building up around me and I could actually *see* young Harry's *petit mal* attacks coming faster and faster as he shuffled around, and I knew he was going to have his big one the next minute, and I began to wonder if I shouldn't stop Cal by grabbing her wrists as if she were some sort of witch making black magic with music—the ward had gone crazy at her arrival, and now she was doing the same damn thing with her Mozart, which was getting louder and louder.

"But just then she modulated triumphantly into the least discordant key and by contrast it sounded like perfect pitch, incredibly right, and at that instant young Harry launched, not into his *grand mal* attack, but into *a weirdly graceful, leaping dance* in perfect time to Cherubino's

Song, and almost before I knew what I was doing I'd taken hold of Miss Craig (whose mouth was open to scream but she wasn't screaming) and was waltzing her around after young Harry—and I could feel the tension in the whole ward around us vanish like smoke. Somehow Cal had *melted* that tension, loosened and unbound it just as she had young Harry's depression, getting him over the hump into safety without his throwing a big fit. It seemed to me at the time to be the nearest thing to magic I've ever seen in my life—witchcraft, all right, but white witchcraft.''

At the words "loosened and unbound," Franz recalled Cal's words that morning about music having "the power to release other things and make them fly and swirl.''

Gun asked, "What happened then?''

"Nothing much, really," Saul said. "Cal kept playing the same tune over and over in the same triumphant key, and we kept on dancing and I think a couple of the others joined in, but she played it a little more softly each time, until it was like music for mice, and then she stopped it and very quietly closed the piano, and we stopped dancing and were smiling at each other, and that was that—except that all of us were in a different place from where we'd started. And a little later she went home without waiting through the shift, as though taking it for granted that what she'd done was something that couldn't possibly be repeated. And we never talked about it much afterwards, she and I. I remember thinking: 'Magic is a one-time thing.' ''

"Say, I like that," Gun said. "I mean the idea of magic—and miracles, too, like those of Jesus, say—and art, too, and history of course—simply being phenomena that *cannot* be repeated. Unlike science, which is all about phenomena that *can* be repeated.''

Franz mused, "Tension *melted* . . . depression loosened and unbound . . . the notes fly upward like the sparks. . . . You know, Gun, that somehow makes me think of what your Shredbasket does that you showed me this morning.''

"Shredbasket?" Saul queried.

Franz briefly explained.

Saul said to Gun, "You never told me about that."

"So?" Gun smiled and shrugged.

"Of course," Franz said, almost regretfully, "the idea of music being good for lunatics and smoothing troubled souls goes way back."

"At least as far as Pythagoras," Gun put in, agreeing. "That's two and a half thousand years."

Saul shook his head decidedly. "This thing Cal did went farther than that."

There was a sharp double knock at the door. Gun opened it.

Fernando looked around the room, bowing politely, then beamed at Franz and said, "E-chess?"

11

FERNANDO WAS A strong player. In Lima he'd had an expert's rating. In Franz's room they divided two rather long, hard-fought games, which were just the thing to occupy fully Franz's dulled evening mind, and during them he became aware of how physically tired his climbing had left him.

From time to time he mused fleetingly about Cal's "white witchcraft" (if it could be called anything like that) and the black sort (even less likely) he'd intruded on at Corona Heights. He wished he'd discussed both incidents at greater length with Saul and Gun, yet doubted they'd have got any further. Oh, well, he'd see them both at the concert tomorrow night—their last words had been of that, asking him to hold seats for them if he came early.

As Fernando departed, the Peruvian pointed at the board and asked, "*Mañana por la noche?*"

That much Spanish Franz understood. He smiled and nodded. If he couldn't play chess again tomorrow night, he could always let Dorotea know.

He slept like the dead and without any remembered dreams.

He awoke completely refreshed, his mind clear and sharp and very calm, his thoughts measured and sure—a good sleep's benison. All of the evening dullness and uncertainty were gone. He remembered each of yesterday's events just as it had happened, but without the emotional overtones of excitement and fear.

The constellation of Orion was shouldering into his window, telling him dawn was near. Its nine brightest stars made an angular, tilted hourglass, challenging the smaller, slenderer one made by the nineteen winking red lights of the TV tower.

He made himself a small, quick cup of coffee with the very hot water from the tap, then put on slippers and robe and took up his binoculars and went very quietly to the roof. All his sensations were sharp. The black windows of the shafts and the black knobless doors of the disused closets stood out as distinctly as the doors of the occupied rooms and the old banisters, many times repainted, he touched as he climbed.

In the room on the roof his small flashlight showed the gleaming cables, the dark, hunched electric motor, and the coldly bunched small, silent iron arms of the relays that would wake violently, and make a great sudden noise, swinging and snapping, if someone pressed an electric button below. The green dwarf and the spider.

Outside, the night wind was bracing. Passing a shaft, he paused and on an impulse dropped a grain of gravel down it. The small sharp sound with its faint hollow overtones from the sheet-iron lining was almost three seconds, he judged, in coming back to him from the bottom. About eighty feet, that was right. There was satisfaction in thinking of how he was awake and clearheaded while so many were still dead asleep.

He looked up at the stars studding the dark dome of night like tiny silver nails. For San Francisco with its fogs and mists, and the invasive smog from Oakland and San Jose, it was a good night for seeing. The gibbous moon had set. He studied lovingly the superconstellation of very bright stars he called the Shield, a sky-spanning hexagon with its corners marked by Capella toward the north, bright Pollux (with Castor near and these years Saturn, too), Procyon the little dogstar, Sirius brightest of all, Bluish Rigel in Orion, and (swinging north again) red-gold Aldebaran. Bringing his binoculars into play, he scanned the golden swarm of the Hyades about that last and then quite close beside the Shield, the tiny bluish-white dipper of the Pleiades.

The sure and steady stars fitted the mood of his morning mind and reinforced it. He looked again at tilted Orion, then dropped his gaze to the red-flashing TV tower. Below it, Corona Heights was a black hump amongst the city's lights.

The memory came to him (a crystal-clear drop, as memories came to him these days in the hour after waking) of how when he'd first seen the TV tower at night, he'd thought of a line from Lovecraft's story, "The Haunter of the Dark," where the watcher of another ill-omened hill (Federal, in Providence) sees "the red Industrial Trust beacon had blazed up to make the night grotesque." When he'd first seen the tower he'd thought it worse than grotesque, but now—how strange!—it had become almost as reassuring to him as starry Orion.

"The Haunter of the Dark!" he thought with a quiet laugh. Yesterday he had lived through a section of a story that might fittingly be called "The Lurker at the Summit." How very strange!

Before returning to his room he briefly surveyed the dark rectangles and skinny pyramid of the downtown skyscrapers—old Thibaut's bugaboos!—the tallest of them with their own warning red lights.

He made himself more coffee, this time using the hot plate and adding sugar and half-and-half. Then he settled himself in bed, determined to use his morning mind to clarify matters that had grown cloudy last evening. Thibaut's drab book and the washed-out tea-rose journal already made the head of his colorful Scholar's Mistress lying beside him on the inside. To them he added the thick black rectangles of Lovecraft's *The Outsider* and the *Collected Ghost Stories* of Montague Rhodes James, and also several yellowed old copies of *Weird Tales* (some puritan had torn their lurid covers off) containing stories by Clark Ashton Smith, shifting some bright magazines to the floor to make room, and the colorful napkins with them.

"You're fading, dear," he told her gaily in his

thoughts, "putting on somber hues. Are you getting dressed for a funeral?"

Then for a space he read more systematically in *Megapolisomancy*. My God, the old boy certainly could do a sort of scholarly-flamboyant thing quite well. Consider:

At any particular time of history there have always been one or two cities of the monstrous sort—*viz.*, Babel or Babylon, Ur-Lhassa, Nineveh, Syracuse, Rome, Samarkand, Tenochtitlan, Peking—but we live in the Megapolitan (or Necropolitan) Age, when such disastrous blights are manifold and threaten to conjoin and enshroud the world with funebral yet multipotent city-stuff. We need a Black Pythagoras to spy out the evil lay of our monstrous cities and their foul shrieking songs, even as the White Pythagoras spied out the lay of the heavenly spheres and their crystalline symphonies, two and a half millennia ago.

Or, adding thereto more of his own brand of the occult:

Since we modern city-men already dwell in tombs, inured after a fashion to mortality, the possibility arises of the indefinite prolongation of this life-in-death. Yet, although quite practicable, it would be a most morbid and dejected existence, without vitality or even thought, but only paramentation, our chief companions paramental entities of azoic origin more vicious than spiders or weasels.

Now what would paramentation be like? Franz wondered. Trance? Opium dreams? Dark, writhing phantoms born of sensory deprivation? Or something entirely different?

Or:

The electro-mephitic city-stuff whereof I speak has potencies for achieving vast effects at distant times and localities, even in the far future and on other orbs, but of the manipulations required for the production and control of such I do not intend to discourse in these pages.

As the overworked yet vigorous current exclamation had it, *wow!* Franz picked up one of the old crumble-edged pulps and was tempted to read Smith's marvelous fantasy, "The City of the Singing Flame," in which great looming metropolises move about and give battle to each other, but he resolutely set it aside for the journal.

Smith (he was sure it was he) had certainly been greatly impressed by de Castries (must be he also), as well he might have been almost fifty years ago. And he had clearly read *Megapolisomancy*, too. It occurred to Franz that this copy was most likely Smith's. Here was a typical passage in the journal:

Three hours today at 607 Rhodes with the furious Tybalt. All I could take. Half the time railing at his fallen-off acolytes, the other half contemptuously tossing me scraps of paranatural truth. But what scraps! That bit about the significance of diagonal streets! How that old devil sees into cities and their invisible sicknesses—a new Pasteur, but of the dead-alive.

He says his book is kindergarten stuff, but the new thing—the core and why of it and how to work it—he keeps only in his mind and in the Grand Cipher he's so sly about. He sometimes calls it (the Cipher) his Fifty-Book, that is, if I'm right and they are the same. Why fifty?

I should write Howard about it, he'd be astounded and—yes!—transfigured, it so agrees with and *illuminates* the decadent and putrescent horror he finds in New York City and Boston and even Providence (not Levantines and Mediterraneans, but half-sensed paramentals!). But I'm not sure he could take it. For that matter, I'm not sure how much more of it I can take myself. And if I so much as hint to old Tiberius at sharing his paranatural knowledge with other kindred spirits, he grows as ugly as his namesake in his last Caprian days and goes back to excoriating those whom he feels failed and betrayed him in the Hermetic Order he created.

I should get out myself—I've all that I can use and there are stories crying to be written. But can I give up the ultimate ecstasy of knowing each day I'll hear from the very lips of Black Pythagoras some new paranatural truth? It's like a drug I have to have. Who can give up such fantasy?—especially when —*the fantasy is the truth*

The paranatural, only a word—*but what it signifies!* The supernatural—a dream of grandmothers and priest and horror writers. But the *paranatural!* Yet how much can I take? Could I stand full contact with a paramental entity and not crack up?

Coming back today, I felt that my senses were metamorphosing. San Francisco was a meganecropolis vibrant with paramentals on the verge of vision and of audition, each block a surreal cenotaph that would bury Dali, and I one of the living dead aware of everything with cold delight. But now I am afraid of this room's walls!

Franz glanced with a chuckle at the drab wall next to the inside of the bed and below the spiderwebby drawing of the TV tower on fluorescent red, remarking to his Scholar's Mistress lying between them, "He certainly was worked up about it, wasn't he, dear?"

Then his face grew intent again. The "Howard" in the entry had to be Howard Phillips Lovecraft, that twentieth-century puritanic Poe from Providence, with his regrettable but undeniable loathing of the immigrant swarms he felt were threatening the traditions and monuments of his beloved New England and the whole Eastern seaboard. (And hadn't Lovecraft done some ghost-writing for a man with a name like Castries? Caster? Carswell?) He and

Smith had been close friends by correspondence. While the mention of a Black Pythagoras was pretty well enough by itself to prove that the keeper of the journal had read de Castrie's book. And those references to a Hermetic Order and a Grand Cipher (or Fifty-Book) teased the imagination. But Smith (who else?) had clearly been as much terrified as fascinated by the ramblings of his crabbed mentor. It showed up even more strikingly in a later entry.

Hated what gloating Tiberius hinted today about the disappearance of Bierce and the deaths of Sterling and Jack London. Not only that they were suicides (which I categorically deny, particularly in the case of Sterling!) but that there were other elements in their deaths—elements for which the old devil appears *to take credit.*

He positively sniggered as he said, "You can be sure of one thing, my dear boy, that all of them had a very rough time *paramentally* before they were snuffed out, or shuffled off to their gray paranatural hells. Very distressing, but it's the common fate of Judases—and little busybodies," he added, glaring at me from under his tangled white eyebrows.

Could he be hypnotising me?

Why do I linger on, now that the menaces outweigh the revelations? That disjointed stuff about techniques of giving paramental entities the scent— clearly a threat.

Franz frowned. He knew quite a bit about the brilliant literary group centered in San Francisco at the turn of the century and of the strangely large number of them who had come to tragic ends—among those, the macabre writer Ambrose Bierce vanishing in revolution-torn Mexico in 1913, London dying of uremia and morphine poisoning a little later, and the fantasy poet Sterling perishing of poison in the 1920s. He reminded himself to ask Jaime Donaldus Byers more about the whole business at the first opportunity.

The final diary entry, which broke off in the middle of a sentence, was in the same vein:

> Today surprised Tiberius making entries in black ink in a ledger of the sort used for bookkeeping. His Fifty-Book? The Grand Cipher? I glimpsed a solid page of what looked like astronomical and astrological symbols (Could there be fifty such?) before he snapped it shut and accused me of spying. I tried to get him off the topic, but he would talk of nothing else.
>
> Why do I stay? The man is a genius (paragenius?) but he's also a paranoiac!
>
> He shook the ledger at me, cackling, "Perhaps you should sneak in some night on those quiet little feet of yours and steal it! Yes, why not do that? It would merely mean your finish, paramentally speaking! That wouldn't hurt. Or would it?"
>
> Yes, by God, it is time I

Franz riffled through the next few pages, all blank, and then gazed over them at the window, which from the bed showed only the equally blank wall of the nearer of the two high rises. It occurred to him what an eerie fantasia of *buildings* all this was: de Castries's ominous theories about them, Smith seeing San Francisco as a . . . yes, mega-necropolis, Lovecraft's horror of the swarming towers of New York, the downtown skyscrapers seen from the roof here, the sea of roofs he'd scanned from Corona Heights, and this beaten old building itself, with its dark halls and yawning lobby, strange shafts and closets, black windows and hiding holes.

12

FRANZ MADE HIMSELF more coffee—it had been full day-light now for some time—and lugged back to bed with him an armful of books from the shelves by his desk. To make room for them, more of the colorful recreational reading had to go on the floor. He joked with his Scholar's Mistress, "You 're growing darker and more intellectual, my dear, but not a day older and as slim as ever. How do you manage it?"

The new books were a fair sampling of what he thought of as his reference library of the really eerie. Mostly not the new occult stuff, which tended to be the work of charlatans and hacks out for the buck, or naive self-deceivers innocent even of scholarship—flotsam and froth on the rising tide of witchcraft (which Franz was also skeptical about)—but books which approached the weird obliquely yet from far firmer footings. He leafed about in them swiftly, intently, quite delightedly, as he sipped his steaming coffee. There was Prof. D.M. Nostig's *The Subliminal Occult*, that curious, intensely skeptical book which rigorously disposes of all claims of the learned parapsychologists and still finds a residue of the inexplic-able; Montague's witty and profound monograph *White Tape*, with its thesis that civilization is being asphyx-iated, mummy-wrapped by its own records, bureaucratic and otherwise, and by its infinitely recessive self-observa-tions; precious, dingy copies of those two extremely rare, slim books thought spurious by many critics—*Ames et Fantômes de Douleur* by the Marquis de Sade and *Knochenmädchen in Pelze mit Peitsche* by Sacher-

Masoch; Oscar Wilde's *De Profundis* and *Suspiria de
Profundis* (with its Three Ladies of Sorrow) by Thomas
De Quincey, that old opium-eater and metaphysician,
both commonplace books but strangely linked by more
than their titles; *The Mauritzius Case* by Jacob Wasser-
man; *Journey to the End of the Night* by Céline; several
copies of Bonewits's periodical *Gnostica*; *The Spider
Glyph in Time* by Mauricio Santos-Lobos; and the monumental *Sex, Death and Supernatural Dread* by Ms.
Frances D. Lettland, Ph.B.

For a long space his morning mind darted about happily
in the eerie wonder-world evoked and buttressed by these
books and de Castries's and the journal and by clear-cut
memories of yesterday's rather strange experiences. Truly, modern cities were the world's supreme mysteries,
and skyscrapers their secular cathedrals.

Scanning the "Ladies of Sorrow" prose poem in *Suspiria*, he wondered not for the first time, whether those
creations of De Quincey had anything to do with Chris-
tianity. True, *Mater Lachrymarum*, Our Lady of Tears,
the eldest sister, did remind one of *Mater Dolorosa*, a
name of the Virgin; and the second sister too, *Mater
Suspiriorum*, Our Lady of Sighs—and even the terrible
and youngest sister, *Mater Tenebrarum*, Our Lady of
Darkness. (De Quincey had intended to write a whole
book about her, *The Kingdom of Darkness*, but apparently never had—*that* would have been something, now!)
But no, their antecedents were in the classical world (they
paralleled the three Fates and the three Furies) and in the
labyrinths of the English laudanum-drinker's drug-wi-
dened awareness.

Meanwhile his intentions were firming as to how he'd
spend this day, which promised to be a beauty, too. First,
start pinning down that elusive 607 Rhodes, beginning by
getting the history of this anonymous building, 811
Geary. It would make an excellent test case—and Cal, as
well as Gun, had wanted to know. Next, go to Corona
Heights again to check out whether he'd really seen his
own window from there. Sometime in the afternoon visit

Jaime Donaldus Byers. (Call him first.) Tonight, of course, Cal's concert.

He blinked and looked around. Despite the open window, the room was full of smoke. With a sorry laugh he carefully stubbed out his cigarette on the edge of the heaped ashtray.

The phone rang. It was Cal, inviting him down to late breakfast. He showered and shaved and dressed and went.

13

IN THE DOORWAY Cal looked so sweet and young in a green dress, her hair in a long pony tail, that he wanted to grab and kiss her. But she also still had on her rapt, meditative look—"Keep intact for Bach."

She said, "Hello, dear. I actually slept those twelve hours I threatened to in my pride. God is merciful. Do you mind eggs again? It's really brunchtime. Pour yourself coffee."

"Any more practice today?" he asked, glancing toward the electronic keyboard.

"Yes, but not with that. This afternoon I'll have three or four hours with the concert harpsichord. And I'll be tuning it."

He drank creamed coffee and watched the poetry of motion as she dreamily broke eggs, an unconscious ballet of white ovoids and slender key-flattened fingertips. He found himself comparing her to Daisy, and, to his amusement, to his Scholar's Mistress. Cal and the latter were both slender, somewhat intellectual, rather silent types, touched with the White Goddess definitely, dreamy but disciplined. Daisy had been touched with the White Goddess too, a poet, and also disciplined, keeping herself intact . . . for brain cancer. He veered off from that.

But White was certainly Cal's adjective; all right, no Lady of Darkness, but a Lady of Light and in eternal opposition to the other, yang to its yin, Ormadz to its Ahriman—yes, by Robert Ingersoll!

And she really did look such a schoolgirl, her face a mask of gay innocence and good behavior. But then he

72

remembered her as she had launched into the first piece of a concert. He'd been sitting up close and a little to one side so that he had seen her full profile. As if by some swift magic, she had become someone he'd never seen before and wasn't sure for a moment he wanted to. Her chin had tucked down into her neck, her nostril had flared, her eye had become all-seeing and merciless, her lips had pressed together and turned down at the corners quite nastily, like a savage schoolmistress, and it had been as if she had been saying, "Now hear me, all you strings and *Mister* Chopin. You behave perfectly now, or else!" It had been the look of the young professional.

"Eat them while they're hot," Cal murmured, slipping his plate in front of him. "Here's the toast. Buttered, somehow."

After a while she asked, "How did you sleep?"

He told her about the stars.

She said, "I'm glad you worship."

"Yes, that's true in a way," he had to admit. "Saint Copernicus, at any rate, and Isaac Newton."

"My father used to swear by them, too," she told him. "Even, I remember once, by Einstein. I started to do it myself too, but Mother gently discouraged me. She thought it tomboyish."

Franz smiled. He didn't bring up this morning's reading or yesterday's events; they seemed wrong topics for now.

It was she who said, "I thought Saul was quite cute last night. I like the way he flirts with Dorotea."

"He loves to pretend to shock her," Franz said.

"And she loves to pretend to be shocked," Cal agreed. "I think I'll give her a fan for Christmas, just to have the delight of watching her manage it. I'm not sure I'd trust him with Bonita, though."

"What, our Saul?" he asked, in only half-pretended astonishment. The memory came, vividly and uncomfortably, of laughter overheard on the stairs yesterday morning, a laughter alive with touching and tickling.

"People have unexpected sides," she observed placidly. "You're very brisk and brimming with energy this morning. Almost bumptious, except you're being considerate for my mood. But underneath you're thoughtful. What are your plans for today?"

He told her.

"That sounds good," she said. "I've heard Byers's place is quite spooky. Or maybe they meant exotic. And I'd really like to find out about 607 Rhodes. You know—peer over the shoulder of 'stout Cortez' and see it there, whatever it is, 'silent upon a peak in Darien.' And just find out the history of this building, like Gun was wondering. That would be fascinating. Well, I should be getting ready."

"Will I see you before? Take you there?" he asked as he got up.

"No, not before, I think," she said thoughtfully. "But afterward." She smiled at him. "I'm relieved to hear you'll be there. Take care, Franz."

"You take care too, Cal," he told her.

"On concert days I wrap myself in wool. No, wait."

She came toward him, head lifted, continuing to smile. He got his arms around her before they kissed. Her lips were soft and cool.

14

AN HOUR LATER, a pleasantly grave young man in the Recorder's Office at City Hall informed Franz that 811 Geary Street was designated Block 320, Lot 23 in his province.

"For anything about the lot's previous history," he said, "you'd have to go to the Assessor's Office. They would know because they handle taxes."

Franz crossed the wide, echoing marble corridor with its ceiling two stories high to the Assessor's Office, which flanked the main entrance to City Hall on the other side. The two great civic guards and idols, he thought, papers and moneys.

A worried woman with graying red hair told him, "Your next step is to go to the Office of Building Permits in the City Hall Annex across the street to your left when you go out, and find when a permit to build on the lot was applied for. When you bring us that information, we can help you. It should be easy. They won't have to go back far. Everything in that area went down in 1906."

Franz obeyed, thinking that all this was becoming not just a fantasia but a ballet of buildings. Investigating just one modest building had led him into what you could call this Courtly Minuet of the Runaround. Doubtless the bothersome public was supposed to get bored and give up at this point, but he'd fool 'em! The brimming spirits Cal had noticed in him were still high.

Yes, a national ballet of all buildings great and small, skyscrapers and shacks, all going up and haunting our streets and cross streets for a while and then eventually coming down, whether helped by earthquakes or not, to the tune of ownership, money, and records, with a symphony orchestra of millions of clerks and bureaucrats, papermen all, each intently reading and obediently tootling his scrap of the infinite score, which itself would all be fed, as the buildings tumbled, into the document-shredding machines, ranks upon ranks of them like banks of violins, not Stradivariuses but Shredmasters. And over everything the paper snow.

In the annex, a businesslike building with low ceilings, Franz was pleasantly surprised (but his cynicism rather dashed) when a portly young Chinaperson, upon being properly supplicated with the ritual formula of numbered block and lot, within two minutes handed him a folded old printed form filled in with ink that had turned brown and which began "Application for Permit to erect a 7-story Brick Building with Steel Frame on the south side of Geary Street 25 feet west of Hyde Street at Estimated Cost of $74,870.00 for Use as a Hotel," and ended with "Filed Jul 15, 1925."

His first thought was that Cal and the others would be relieved to hear that the building apparently had a steel frame—a point they'd wondered about during earthquake speculations and to which they'd never been able to get a satisfactory answer. His second was that the date made the building almost disappointingly recent—the San Francisco of Dashiell Hammett . . . and Clark Ashton Smith. Still, the big bridges hadn't been built then; ferries did all their work. Fifty years was a respectable age.

He copied out most of the brown-ink stuff, returned the application to the stout young man (who smiled, hardly inscrutably), and footed it back to the Assessor's Office, swinging his briefcase jauntily. The red-haired woman was worrying elsewhere, and two ancient men who both limped received his information dubiously, but finally deigned to consult a computer, joking together as to whether it would work, but clearly reverent for all their humor.

One of them pushed some buttons and read off from a

screen invisible to the public, "Yep, permit granted September nine, 1925, and built in '26. Construction completed Jun—June."

"They said it was for use as a hotel," Franz asked. "Could you tell me what name?"

"For that you'd have to consult a city directory for the year. Ours don't go back that far. Try in the public library across the square."

Franz dutifully crossed the wide gray expanse, dark green with little segregated trees and bright with small gushing fountains and two long pools rippling in the wind. On all four sides the civic buildings stood pompously, most of them blocky and nondescript, but City Hall behind him with its greenish dome and classic cupola and the main public library ahead somewhat more decorated, the latter with names of great thinkers and American writers, which (score one for our side) included Poe. While a block north the darkly severe and wholly modern (all glass) Federal Building loomed up like a watchful elder brother.

Feeling ebullient and now a bit lucky, too, Franz hurried. He still had much to do today and the high sun said it was getting on. Inside the swinging doors he angled through the press of harsh young women with glasses, children, belted hippies, and cranky old men (typical readers all), returned two books, and without waiting for an okay, he took the elevator to the empty corridor of the third floor. In the hushed, rather elegant San Francisco Room a slightly precious lady whispered to him that her city directories went up only to 1918, the later (more common?) ones were in the main catalog room on the second floor with the phone books.

Feeling slightly deflated and a bit run-around again, but not much, Franz descended to the big, fantastically high-ceilinged familiar room. In the last century and the early years of this, libraries had been built in the same spirit as banks and railroad stations—all pomp and pride. In a corner partitioned off by high, packed shelves, he found the rows of books he wanted. His hand went toward the

1926, then shifted to the 1927—that would be sure to list the hotel, if there had been one. Now for some fun—looking up the addresses of everyone mentioned in the application and finding the hotel itself, of course, though that last would take some hunting, have to check the addresses (which might be given by cross streets rather than numbers) of all the hotels—and maybe of the apartment hotels, too.

Before seating himself he glanced at his wristwatch. My God, it was later than he'd thought. If he didn't make up some time, he'd arrive at Corona Heights after the sun had left the slot and so too late for the experiment he intended. And books like this didn't circulate.

He took only a couple of seconds coming to a decision. After a casual but searching look all around to make sure no one was watching him at the moment, he thrust the directory into his deep briefcase and marched out of the catalog room, picking up a couple of paperbacks at random from one of the revolving wire stands set here and there. Then he tramped softly and measuredly down the great marble stairs that were wide and lofty and long and broad-stepped enough for a triumph in a Roman film epic, feeling all eyes upon him but hardly believing that. He stopped at the desk to check out the two paperbacks and drop them ostentatiously into his briefcase, and then walked out of the building without a glance at the guard, who never did look into briefcases and bags (so far as Franz had noticed) provided he'd seen you check out some books at the desk.

Franz seldom did that sort of thing, but today's promise seemed to make it worth taking little risks.

There was a 19-Polk coming outside. He caught it, thinking somewhat complacently that now he had successfully become one of Saul's kleptomaniacs. Heigh-ho for the compulsive life!

15

At 811 Franz glanced at his mail (nothing worth opening right away) and then looked around the room. He'd left the transom open. Dorotea was right—a thin, athletic person could crawl through it. He shut it. Then he leaned out the open casement window and checked each way—to either side and up (one window like his, then the roof) and down (Cal's two below and, three below that, the shaft's grimy bottom, a cul-de-sac, scattered with junk fallen over the years). There was no way anyone could reach this window short of using ladders. But he noticed that his bathroom window was only a short step away from the window of the next apartment on this floor. He made sure it was locked.

Then he took off the wall the big spidery black sketch of the TV tower that was almost entirely bright fluorescent red background and securely wedged and thumbtacked it, red side out, in the open casement window, using drawing pins. There! that would show up unmistakably from Corona in the sunlight when it came.

Next he put on a light sweater under his coat (it seemed a bit chillier than yesterday) and stuck an extra pack of cigarettes in his pocket. He didn't pause to make himself a sandwich (after all, he'd had *two* pieces of toast this morning at Cal's). At the last minute he remembered to stuff his binoculars and map into his pocket, *and* Smith's journal; he might want to refer to it at Byers's. (He'd called the man up earlier and gotten a typically effusive but somewhat listless invitation to drop in any time after the middle of the afternoon and stay if he liked for the little

79

party coming up in the evening. Some of the guests would be in costume, but costume was not mandatory.)

As a final touch he placed the 1927 city directory where his Scholar's Mistress's rump would be, and giving it a quick intimate caress, said flippantly, "There, my dear, I've made you a receiver of stolen property; but don't worry, you're going to give it back."

Then without further leavetaking, or any send-off at all, he double-locked the door behind him and was away into the wind and sunlight.

At the corner there was no bus coming, so he started to walk the eight short blocks to Market, striding briskly. At Ellis he deliberately devoted a few seconds to looking at (worshiping?) his favorite tree in San Francisco: a six-story candlestick pine, guyed by some thin strong wires, waving its green fingers over a brown wooden wall trimmed with yellow between two taller buildings in a narrow lot the high-rise moguls had somehow overlooked. Inefficient bastards!

A block farther on, the bus overtook him and he got aboard—it would save a minute. Transferring to the N-Judah car at Market, he got a start (and had to sidestep swiftly) when a pallid drunk in a shapeless, dirty pale gray suit (but no shirt) came staggering diagonally from nowhere (and apparently bound for the same place). He thought, "There but for the grace of God, et cetera," and veered off from those thoughts, as he had at Cal's from the memories of Daisy's mortal disease.

In fact, he banished all dark stuff so well from his mind that the creaking car seemed to mount Market and then Duboce in the bright sunlight like the victorious general's chariot in a Roman triumph. (Should he be painted red and have a slave at his elbow reminding him continuously in a low voice that he was mortal?—a charming fancy!) He swung off at the tunnel's mouth and climbed dizzying Duboce, breathing deeply. It seemed not quite so steep today, or else he was fresher. (And always easier to climb up than down—if you had wind enough!—the mountaineering experts said.) The neighborhood looked particularly neat and friendly.

At the top a young couple hand in hand (lovers, quite obviously) were entering the dappling shades and green glooms of Buena Vista Park. Why had the place seemed so sinister yesterday? Some other day he'd follow in their path to the park's pleasantly wooded summit and then stroll leisurely down the other side into the festive Haight, that overrated menace! With Cal and perhaps the others—the picnic Saul'd suggested.

But today his was another voyage—he had other business. Pressing business, too. He glanced at his wristwatch and stepped along smartly, barely pausing for the fine view of the Heights jaggedy crest from the top of Park Hill. Soon he was going through the little gate in the high wire fence and across the green field back of the brown-sloped Heights with their rocky crown. To his right, two little girls were supervising a sort of dolls' tea party on the grass. Why, they were the girls he'd seen running yesterday. And just beyond them their Saint Bernard was stretched out beside a young woman in faded blue denim, who was kneading his loose, thickly furred mane as she combed her own long blonde hair.

While to the left, two Dobermans—the same two, by God!—were stretched out and yawning beside another young couple lying close together though not embracing. As Franz smiled at them, the man smiled back and waved a casual greeting. It really was the poet's cliché, "an idyllic scene." Nothing at all like yesterday. Now Cal's suggestion about the dark psionic powers of little girls seemed quite overwrought, even if charming.

He would have lingered, but time was wasting. Got to go to Taffy's house, he thought with a chuckle. He mounted the ragged, gravelly slope—it wasn't all that steep!—with just one breather. Over his shoulder the TV tower stood tall, her colors bright, as fresh and gussied-up and elegant as a brandnew whore (Your pardon, Goddess). He felt fey.

When he got to the corona, he noticed something he
hadn't yesterday. Several of the rock surfaces—at least on
his side—had been scrawled on at past times with dark
and pale and various colored paints from spray cans, most
of it rather weathered now. There weren't so many names
and dates as simple figures. Lopsided five- and six-point-
ed stars, a sunburst, crescents, triangles and squares. And
there a rather modest phallus with a sign beside it like two
parentheses joined—yoni as well as lingam. He thought
of—of all things!—de Castries's Grand Cipher. Yes, he
noted with a grin, there were symbols here that could be
taken as astronom- and/or astrological. Those circles with
crosses and arrows—Venus and Mars. While that horned
disk might be Taurus.

You certainly have odd tastes in interior decoration,
Taffy, he told himself. Now to check if you're stealing my
marrowbone.

Well, spray-painting signs on rocky eminences was
standard practice these progressive youth-oriented days—
the graffiti of the heights. Though he recalled how at the
beginning of the century the black magician Aleister
Crowley had spent a summer painting in huge red capitals
on the Hudson Palisades DO WHAT THOU WILT IS
THE ONLY COMMANDMENT and EVERY MAN
AND WOMAN IS A STAR to shock and instruct New
Yorkers on riverboats. He perversely wondered what gay
sprayed graffiti would have done to the eerie rock-
crowned hills in Lovecraft's "Whisperer in Darkness"
and "Dunwich Horror" or "At the Mountains of Mad-
ness," where the hills were Everests, or Leiber's "A Bit
of the Dark World," for that matter.

He found his stone seat of yesterday and then made
himself smoke a cigarette to give himself time to steady
his nerves and breathing, and relax, although he was
impatient to make sure he'd kept ahead of the sun. Actually he knew he had, though by a rather slender margin. His
wristwatch assured him of that.

If anything, it was clearer and sunnier than yesterday.
The strong west wind was sweeping the air, making itself

felt even in San Jose, which now had no visible pillow of smog over it. The distant little peaks beyond the East Bay cities and north in Marin County stood out quite sharply. The bridges were bright.

Even the sea of roofs itself seemed friendly and calm today. He found himself thinking of the incredible number of lives it sheltered, some seven hundred thousand, while a slightly larger number even than that were employed beneath those roofs—a measure of the vast companies of people brought into San Francisco each day from the metropolitan area by the bridges and the other freeways and by BART under the waters of the Bay.

With unaided eyes he located what he thought was the slot in which his window was—it was full of sun, at any rate—and then got out his binoculars. He didn't bother to string them around his neck—his grip was firm today. Yes, there was the fluorescent red, all right, seeming to fill the whole window, the scarlet stood out so, but then you could tell it just occupied the lower left-hand quarter. Why, he could almost make out the drawing . . . no, that would be too much, those thin black lines.

So much for Gun's (and his own) doubts as to whether he'd located the right window yesterday! It was funny, though, how the human mind would cast doubt even on itself in order to explain away unusual and unconventional things it had seen vividly and unmistakably. It left you in the middle, the human mind did.

But the seeing was certainly exceptionally fine today. How clearly pale yellow Coit Tower on Telegraph Hill, once Frisco's tallest structure, now a trifle, stood out against the blue Bay. And the pale blue gilded globe of Columbus Tower—a perfect antique gem against the ordered window slits of the Transamerica Pyramid that were like perforations in a punchcard. And the high rounded windows of the shipshaped old Hobart Building's stern, that was like the lofty, richly encrusted admiral's cabin of a galleon, against the stark, vertical aluminum lines of the new Wells Fargo Building towering over it like a space-to-space interstellar freighter waiting to blast. He roved the binoculars around, effortlessly refining the focus. Why, he'd been wrong about Grace Cathedral with its darkly suggestive, richly colorful modern stained glass inside. Beside the unimaginative contemporary bulk of Cathedral Apartments you could see its slim, crocketed spire stabbing up like a saw-edged stiletto that carried on its point a small gilded cross.

He took another look into his window slot before the shadow swallowed it. Perhaps he *could* see the drawing if he 'fined the focus. . . .

Even as he watched, the oblong of fluorescent card-board was jerked out of sight. From his window there thrust itself a pale brown thing that wildly waved its long, uplifted arms at him. While low between them he could see its face stretched toward him, a mask as narrow as a ferret's, a pale brown, utterly blank triangle, two points above that might mean eyes or ears, and one ending below in a tapered chin . . . no, snout . . . no, very short trunk— *a questing mouth that looked as if it were for sucking marrow. Then the paramental entity reached through the glasses at his eyes.*

16

IN HIS NEXT instant of awareness, Franz heard a hollow *chunk* and a faint tinkling, and he was searching the dark sea of roofs with his naked eyes to try to locate anywhere a swift pale brown thing stalking him across them and taking advantage of every bit of cover: a chimney and its cap, a cupola, a water tank, a penthouse large or tiny, a thick standpipe, a wind scoop, a ventilator hood, hood of a garbage chute, a skylight, a roof's low walls, the low walls of an airshaft. His heart was pounding and his breathing fast.

His frantic thoughts took another turn and he was scanning the slopes before and beside him, and the cover their rocks and dry bushes afforded. Who knew how fast a paramental traveled? as a cheetah? as sound? as light? It could well be back here on the heights already. He saw his binoculars below the rock against which he'd unintentionally hurled them when he'd thrust out his hands convulsively to keep the thing out of his eyes.

He scrambled to the top. From the green field below the little girls were gone, and their chaperone and the other couple and the three animals. But even as he was noticing that, a large dog (one of the Dobermans? or something else?) loped across it toward him and disappeared behind a clump of rocks at the base of the slope. He'd thought of running down that way, but not if that dog (and what others? and what else?) were on the prowl. There was too much cover on this side of Corona Heights.

He stepped quickly down and stood on his stone seat and made himself hold still and look out squintingly until

he found the slot where his window was. It was full of
darkness, so that even with his binoculars he wouldn't
have been able to see anything.

He dropped down to the path, taking advantage of
handholds, and while shooting rapid looks around, picked
up his broken binoculars and jammed them in his pocket,
though he didn't like the way the loose glass in them
tinkled a little—or the gravel grated under his careful feet,
for that matter. Such small sounds could give away a
person's whereabouts.

One instant of awareness couldn't change your life this
much, could it? But it had.

He tried to straighten out his reality, while not letting
down his guard. To begin with, there were no such things
as paramental entities, they were just part of de Castries's
1890s pseudoscience. But he had *seen* one, and as Saul
had said, there was no reality except an individual's
immediate sensations—vision, hearing, pain, those were
real. Deny your mind, deny your sensations, and you
deny reality. Even to try to rationalize was to deny. But of
course there were false sensations, optical and other illusions. . . . Really, now! Try telling a tiger springing
upon you he's an illusion. Which left exactly hallucina-
tion and, to be sure, insanity. Parts of inner reality
. . . and who was to say how far inner reality went? As
Saul had also said, "Who's going to believe a crazy if he
says he's just seen a ghost? Inner or outer reality? Who's
to tell then?" In any case, Franz told himself, he must
keep firmly in mind that he might now be crazy—without
letting down his guard one bit on that account either!

All the while that he was thinking these thoughts, he
was moving watchfully, carefully, and yet quite rapidly
down the slope, keeping a little off the gravel path so as to
make less noise, ready to leap aside if something rushed
him. He kept darting glances to either side and over his
shoulder, noting points of concealment and the distances
to them. He got the impression that something of considerable size was following him, something that was won-
derfully clever in making its swift moves from one bit of

cover to the next, something of which he saw (or thought he saw) only the edges. One of the dogs? Or more than one? Perhaps urged on by rapt-faced, fleet-footed little girls. Or . . . ? He found himself picturing the dogs as spiders as furry and as big. Once in bed, her limbs and breasts pale in the dawn's first light, Cal had told him a dream in which two big borzois following her had changed into two equally large and elegant creamy-furred spiders.

What if there were an earthquake now (he must be ready for *anything*) and the brown ground opened in smoking cracks and swallowed his pursuers up? And himself, too?

He reached the foot of the crest and soon was circling past the Josephine Randall Junior Museum. His sense of being pursued grew less—or rather of being pursued at such close distance. It was good to be close to human habitations again, even if seemingly empty ones, and even though buildings were objects that things could hide behind. This was the place where they taught the boys and girls not to be afraid of rats and bats and giant tarantulas and other entities. Where were the children anyhow? Had some wise Pied Piper led them all away from this menaced locality? Or had they piled into the "Sidewalk Astronomer" panel truck and taken off for other stars? What with earthquakes and eruptions of large pale spiders and less wholesome entities, San Francisco was no longer very safe. Oh, you fool, watch! watch!

As he left the low building behind him and descended the hillside ramp and went past the tennis courts and finally reached the short dead-end cross street that was the boundary of Corona Heights, his nerves quieted down somewhat and his whirling thoughts, too, though he got a dreadful start when he heard from somewhere a sharp squeal of rubber on asphalt and thought for a moment that the parked car at the other end of the cross street had started for him, steered by its two little tombstone head-rests.

Approaching Beaver Street by way of a narrow public

stairway between two buildings, he had another quick
vision of a local quake behind him and of Corona Heights
convulsed but intact, and then lifting up its great brown
shoulders and rocky head, and shaking the Josephine
Randall Junior Museum off its back, preparatory to stalking down into the city.

As he descended Beaver Street, he began to encounter
people at last; not many, but a few. He remembered as if
from another lifetime his intention to visit Byers (he'd
even phoned) and debated whether to go through with it.
He'd never been here before, his previous meetings in San
Francisco with the man had been at a mutual friend's
apartment in the Haight. Cal had said someone had told
her it was a spooky place, but it didn't look that from the
outside with its fresh olive-green paint and thin gold trim.

His mind was made up for him when an ambulance on
Castro, which he'd just crossed, let loose with its yelping
siren on approaching Beaver, and the foul nerve-twanging
sound growing suddenly unendurably loud as the vehicle
crossed Beaver, fairly catapulted Franz up the steps to the
faintly gold-arabesqued olive door and set him pounding
the bronze knocker that was in the shape of a merman.

He realized that the idea of going somewhere other than
home appealed to him. Home was as dangerous as—
perhaps more dangerous than—Corona Heights.

After a maddeningly long pause the polished brass
knob turned, the door began to open, and a voice grandilo-
quent as that of Vincent Price at his fruitiest said, "Here's
a knocking indeed. Why, it's Franz Westen. Come in,
come in. But you look shaken, my dear Franz, as if that
ambulance had delivered you. What have the wicked,
unpredictable streets done now?"

As soon as Franz was reasonably sure that the neatly
bearded, rather theatric visage was Byers's, he pressed
past him, saying, "Shut the door. I *am* shaken," while he
scanned the richly furnished entry and the large, glamor-
ous room opening from it and the thickly carpeted stairs
ahead going up to a landing mellow with light that had

come through stained glass, and the dark hall beyond the stairs.

Behind him, Byers was saying, "All in good time. There, it's locked, and I've even thrown a bolt, if that makes you feel better. And now some wine? Fortified, your condition would seem to call for. But tell me at once if I should call a doctor, so we won't have that fretting us."

They were facing each other now. Jaime Donaldus Byers was about Franz's age, somewhere in the mid-forties, medium tall, with the easy, proud carriage of an actor. He wore a pale green Nehru jacket faintly embroidered in gold, similar trousers, leather sandals, and a long, pale violet dressing gown, open but belted with a narrow sash. His well-combed auburn hair hung to his shoulders. His Vandyke beard and narrow moustache were neatly trimmed. His palely sallow complexion, noble brow, and large liquid eyes were Elizabethan, suggesting Edmund Spenser. And he was clearly aware of all this.

Franz, whose attention was still chiefly elsewhere, said, "No, no doctor. And no alcohol, this time, Donaldus. But if I could have some coffee, black . . ."

"My dear Franz, at once. Just come with me into the living room. Everything's there. But what is it that has shaken you? What's *chasing* you?"

"I am afraid," Franz said curtly and then added quickly, "of paramentals."

"Oh, is that what they're calling the big menace these days?" Byers said lightly, but his eyes had narrowed sharply first. "I'd always thought it was the Mafia. Or the CIA? Or something from your own 'Weird Underground,' some novelty? And there's always reliable Russia. I am up to date only sporadically. I live *firmly* in the world of art, where reality and fantasy are one."

And he turned and led the way into the living room, beckoning Franz to follow. As he stepped forward, Franz became aware of a melange of scents: freshly brewed coffee, wines and liqueurs, a heavy incense and some sharper perfume. He thought fleetingly of Saul's story of the Invisible Nurse and glanced toward the stairs and back hall, now behind him.

Byers motioned Franz to select a seat, while he busied himself at a heavy table on which stood slender bottles and two small steaming silver urns. Franz recalled Peter Viereck's poetry line, ''Art, like the bartender, is never drunk,'' and briefly recalled the years when bars had been places of refuge for him from the terrors and agonies of the outside world. But this time fear had come inside with him.

17

THE ROOM WAS furnished sybaritically, and while not specifically Arabian, held much more ornamentation than depiction. The wallpaper was of a creamy hue, on which faint gold lines made a pattern of arabesques featuring mazes. Franz chose a larger hassock that was set against a wall and from which he had an easy view of the hall, the rear archway, and the windows, whose faintly glittering curtains transmitted yellowed sunlight and blurred, dully gilded pictures of the outdoors. Silver gleamed from two black shelves beside the hassock and Franz's gaze was briefly held against his will (his fear) by a collection of small statuettes of modish young persons engaged with great hauteur in various sexual activities, chiefly perverse—the style between Art Deco and Pompeiian. Under any other circumstances he would have given them more than a passing scrutiny. They looked incredibly detailed and devilishly expensive. Byers, he knew, came of a wealthy family and produced a sizable volume of exquisite poetry and prose sketches every three or four years.

Now that fortunate person set a thin, large white cup half-filled with steaming coffee and also a steaming silver pot upon a firm low stand by Franz that additionally held an obsidian ashtray. Then he settled himself in a convenient low chair, sipped the pale yellow wine he'd brought, and said, "You said you had some questions when you phoned. About that journal you attribute to Smith and of which you sent me a photocopy."

Franz answered, his gaze still roving systematically.

"That's right. I do have some questions for you. But first I've got to tell you what happened to me just now."

"Of course. By all means. I'm most eager to know."

Franz tried to condense his narrative, but soon found he couldn't do much of that without losing significance, and ended by giving a quite full and chronological account of the events of the past thirty hours. As a result, and with some help from the coffee, which he'd needed, and from his cigarettes, which he'd forgotten to smoke for nearly an hour, he began after a while to feel a considerable catharsis. His nerves settled down a great deal. He didn't find himself changing his mind about what had happened or its vital importance, but having a human companion and sympathetic listener certainly did make a great difference emotionally.

For Byers paid close attention, helping him on by little nods and eye-narrowings and pursing of lips and voiced brief agreements and comments—at least they were mostly brief. True, those last weren't so much practical as aesthetic—even a shade frivolous—but that didn't bother Franz at all, at first, he was so intent on his story; while Byers, even when frivolous, seemed deeply impressed and far more than politely credulous about all Franz told him.

When Franz briefly mentioned the bureaucratic runaround he'd gotten, Byers caught the humor at once, putting in, "Dance of the clarks, how quaint!" And when he heard about Cal's musical accomplishments, he observed, "Franz, you have a sure taste in girls. A harpsichordist! What could be more perfect? My current dear-friend-secretary-playfellow-cohousekeeper-cum-moon-goddess is North Chinese, supremely erudite, and works in precious metal—she did those deliciously vile silvers, cast by the lost-wax process of Cellini. She'd have served you your coffee except it's one of our personal days, when we recreate ourselves apart. I call her Fa Lo Suee (the Daughter of Fu Manchu—it's one of our semi-private jokes) because she gives the delightfully sinister impression of being able to take over the world if ever she chose.

You'll meet her if you stay this evening. Excuse me, please go on.'' And when Franz mentioned the astrological graffiti on Corona Heights, he whistled softly and said, "How *very* appropriate!" with such emphasis that Franz asked him, "Why?" but he responded, "Nothing. I mean the sheer *range* of our tireless defacers. Next: a pyramid of beer cans on Shasta's mystic top. This pear wine is delightful—you should taste it—a supreme creation of the San Martin winery on Santa Clara Valley's sun-kissed slopes. Pray continue.''

But when Franz mentioned *Megapolisomancy* a third or fourth time and even quoted from it, he lifted a hand in interruption and went to a tall bookcase and unlocked it and took from behind the darkly clouded glass a thin book bound in black leather beautifully tooled with silver arabesques and handed it to Franz, who opened it.

It was a copy of de Castries's gracelessly printed book, identical with his own copy, as far as he could tell, save for the binding. He looked up questioningly.

Byers explained, "Until this afternoon I never dreamed you owned a copy, my dear Franz. You showed me only the violet-ink journal, you'll recall, that evening in the Haight, and later sent me a photocopy of the written-on pages. You never mentioned buying another book along with it. And on that evening you were, well . . . rather tiddly.''

"In those days I was drunk all of the time," Franz said flatly.

"I understand . . . poor Daisy . . . say no more. The point is this: *Megapolisomancy* happens to be not only a rare book, but also, literally, a very secret one. In his last years, de Castries had a change of mind about it and tried to hunt down every single copy and burn them all. And did! Almost. He was known to have behaved vindictively toward persons who refused to yield up their copies. He was, in fact, a very nasty and, I would say (except I abhor moral judgments) evil old man. At any rate, I saw no point at the time in telling you that I possessed what I thought then to be the sole surviving copy of the book.''

Franz said, "Thank God! I was hoping you knew something about de Castries."

Byers said, "I know quite a bit. But first, finish your story. You were on Corona Heights, today's visit, and had just looked through your binoculars at the Transamerica Pyramid, which made you quote de Castries on 'our modern pyramids . . .' "

"I will," Franz said, and did it quite quickly, but it was the worst part; it brought vividly back to him his sight of the triangular pale brown muzzle and his flight down Corona Heights, and by the time he was done he was sweating and darting his glance about again.

Byers let out a sigh, then said with relish, "And so you came to me, pursued by paramentals to the very door!" And he turned in his chair to look somewhat dubiously at the blurry golden windows behind him.

"Donaldus!" Franz said angrily, "I'm telling you things that happened, not some damn weird tale I've made up for your entertainment. I know it all hangs on a figure I saw several times at a distance of two miles with seven-power binoculars, and so anyone's free to talk about optical illusions and instrumental defects and the power of suggestion, but I know something about psychology and optics, and it was none of those! I went pretty deeply into the flying-saucer business, and I never once saw or heard of a single UFO that was really convincing—and I've seen haloed highlights on aircraft that were oval-shaped and glowed and pulsed exactly like the ones in half the saucer sightings. But I have no doubts of that sort about what I saw today and yesterday."

But even as he was pouring that out and still uneasily checking the windows and doors and glooms himself, Franz realized that deep down inside he *was* beginning to doubt his memories of what he'd seen—perhaps the human mind was incapable of holding a fear like his for more than about an hour unless it were reinforced by repetition—but he was damned if he'd tell Donaldus so!

He finished icily, "Of course, it's quite possible I've

gone insane, temporarily or permanently, and am 'seeing things,' but until I'm sure of that I'm not going to behave like a reckless idiot—or a hilarious one.''

Donaldus, who had been making protesting and imploring faces at him all the while, now said injuredly and placatingly, ''My *dear* Franz, I never for a moment doubted your seriousness or had the faintest suspicion that you were psychotic. Why, I've been inclined to believe in paramental entities ever since I read de Castries's book, and especially after hearing several circumstantial, very peculiar stories about him, and now your truly shocking eyewitness narrative has swept my last doubts away. But I've not seen one yet—if I did, I'm sure I'd feel all the terror you do and more—but until then, and perhaps in any case, and despite the proper horror they evoke in us, they are most *fascinating* entities, don't you agree? Now as for thinking your account a tale or story, my dear Franz, to be a good story is to me the highest test of the truth of anything. I make no distinction whatever between reality and fantasy, or the objective and the subjective. All life and all awareness are ultimately one, including intensest pain and death itself. Not all the play need please us, and ends are never comforting. Some things fit together harmoniously and beautifully and startlingly with thrilling discords—those are true—and some do not, and those are merely bad art. Don't you see?''

Franz had no immediate comment. He certainly hadn't given de Castries's book the least credence by itself, but . . . He nodded thoughtfully, though hardly in answer to the question. He wished for the sharp minds of Gun and Saul . . . and Cal.

''And now to tell you *my* story,'' Donaldus said, quite satisfied. ''But first a touch of brandy—that seems called for. And you? Well, some hot coffee then, I'll fetch it. And a few biscuits? Yes.''

Franz had begun to feel headachy and slightly nauseated. The plain arrowroot cookies, barely sweet, seemed to help. He poured himself coffee from the fresh pot, adding some of the cream and sugar his host had thoughtfully brought this time. It helped, too. He didn't relax his watchfulness, but he began to feel more comfortable in it, as if the awareness of danger were becoming a way of life.

18

DONALDUS LIFTED A a finger with a ring of silver filigree on it and said, "You have to keep in mind de Castries died when I (and you) were infants. Almost all my information comes from a couple of the not-so-close and hardly well-beloved friends of de Castries's last declining years: George Ricker, who was a locksmith and played *go* with him, and Herman Klaas, who ran a secondhand bookstore on Turk Street and was a sort of romantic anarchist and for a while a Technocrat. And a bit from Clark Ashton Smith. Ah, that interests you, doesn't it? It was only a bit—Clark didn't like to talk about de Castries. I think it was because of de Castries and his theories that Clark stayed away from big cities, even San Francisco, and became the hermit of Auburn and Pacific Grove. And I've got some data from old letters and clippings, but not much. People didn't like to write down things about de Castries, and they had reasons, and in the end the man himself made secrecy a way of life. Which is odd, considering that he began his chief career by writing and publishing a sensational book. Incidentally, I got my copy from Klaas when he died, and he may have found it among de Castries's things after de Castries died—I was never sure.

"Also," Donaldus continued, "I'll probably tell the story—at least in spots—in a somewhat poetic style. Don't let that put you off. It merely helps me organize my thoughts and select the significant items. I won't be straying in the least from the strict truth as I've discovered it;

though there may be traces of paramentals in my story, I suppose, and certainly one ghost. I think all modern cities, especially the crass, newly built, highly industrial ones, should have ghosts. They are a civilizing influence.''

19

DONALDUS TOOK A generous sip of brandy, rolled it around on his tongue appreciatively, and settled back in his chair.

"In 1900, as the century turned," he began dramatically, "Thibaut de Castries came to sunny, lusty San Francisco like a dark portent from realms of cold and coal smoke in the East that pulsed with Edison's electricity and from which thrust Sullivan's steel-framed skyscrapers. Madame Curie had just proclaimed radioactivity to the world, and Marconi radio spanning the seas. Madam Blavatsky had brought eerie theosophy from the Himalayas and passed on the occult torch to Annie Besant. The Scottish Astronomer-Royal Piazzi Smith had discovered the history of the world and its ominous future in the Grand Gallery of the Great Pyramid of Egypt. While in the law courts, Mary Baker Eddy and her chief female accolytes were hurling accusations of witchcraft and black magic at each other. Spencer preached science. Ingersoll thundered against superstition. Freud and Jung were plunging into the limitless dark of the subconscious. Wonders undreamed had been unveiled at the Universal Exhibition in Paris, for which the Eiffel tower had been built, and the World's Columbian Exposition in Chicago. New York was digging her subways. In South Africa the Boers were firing at the British Krupp's field guns of unburstable steel. In far Cathay the Boxers raged, deeming themselves invulnerable to bullets by their magic. Count von Zeppelin was launching his first dirigible airship, while the Wright Brothers were readying for their first flight.

"De Castries brought with him only a large black Gladstone bag stuffed with copies of his ill-printed book that he could no more sell than Melville his *Moby Dick*, and a skull teeming with galvanic, darkly illuminating ideas, and (some insist) a large black panther on a leash of

German silver links. And, according to still others, he was also accompanied or else pursued by a mysterious, tall, slender woman who always wore a black veil and loose dark dresses that were more like robes, and had a way of appearing and disappearing suddenly. In any case, de Castries was a wiry, tireless, rather small black eagle of a man, with piercing eyes and sardonic mouth, who wore his glamour like an opera cape.

"There were a dozen legends of his origins. Some said he improvised a new one each night, and some that they were all invented by others solely on the inspiration of his darkly magnetic appearance. The one that Klaas and Ricker most favored was moderately spectacular: that as a boy of thirteen during the Franco-Prussian War he had escaped from besieged Paris by hydrogen balloon along with his mortally wounded father, who was an explorer of darkest Africa; his father's beautiful and learned young Polish mistress; and a black panther (an earlier one) which his father had originally captured in the Congo and which they had just rescued from the zoological gardens, where the starving Parisians were slaughtering the wild animals for food. (Of course, another legend had it that at that time he was a boy aide-de-camp to Garibaldi in Sicily and his father the most darkly feared of the Carbonari.)

"Rapidly travelling southeast across the Mediterranean, the balloon encountered at midnight an electrical tempest which added to its velocity but also forced it down nearer and nearer to the white-fanged waves. Picture the scene as revealed by almost continuous lightning flashes in the frail and overweighted gondola. The panther crouched back into one side, snarling and spitting, lashing his tail, his claws dug deeply into the wickerwork with a strength that threatened to rend it. The faces of the dying father (an old hawk), the earnest and flashing-eyed boy (already a young eagle), and the proud, intellectual, fiercely loyal, brooding girl—all of them desperate and pale as death in the lightning's bluish glare. While thunder resounded deafeningly, as if the black atmosphere were being ripped, or great artillery pieces let off at their ears.

Suddenly the rain tasted salt on their wet lips—spray from the hungry waves.

"The dying father grasped the right hands of the two others, joined them together, gripped them briefly with his own, gasped a few words (they were lost in the gale) and with a final convulsive burst of strength hurled himself overboard.

"The balloon leaped upward out of the storm and raced on southeast. The chilled, terrorized, but undaunted young people huddled together in each other's arms. From across the gondola the black panther, subsiding, stared at them with enigmatic green eyes. While in the southeast, toward which they were speeding, the horned moon appeared above the clouds, like the witch-crown of the Queen of Night, setting her seal upon the scene.

"The balloon landing in the Egyptian desert near Cairo, young de Castries plunged at once into a study of the Great Pyramid, assisted by his father's young Polish mistress (now his own), and by the fact that he was maternally descended from Champollion, decipherer of the Rosetta Stone. He made all Piazzi Smith's discoveries (and a few more besides, which he kept secret) ten years in advance and laid the basis for his new science of supercities (and also his Grand Cipher) before leaving Egypt to investigate mega-structures and cryptoglyphics (he called it) and paramentality throughout the world."

"You know, that link with Egypt fascinates me," Byers said parenthetically as he poured himself more brandy. "It makes me think of Lovecraft's Nyarlathotep, who came out of Egypt to deliver pseudoscientific lectures heralding the crumbling away of the world."

Mention of Lovecraft reminded Franz of something. He interjected, "Say, didn't Lovecraft have a revision client with a name like Thibaut de Castries?"

Byers' eyes widened. "He did indeed. Adolphe De Castro."

"That much alike! You don't suppose . . . ?"

". . . that they were the same person?" Byers smiled. "The possibility has occurred to me, my dear Franz, and

there is this additionally to be said for the idea: that
Lovecraft variously referred to Adolphe De Castro as 'an
amiable charlatan' and 'an unctuous old hypocrite' (he
paid Lovecraft for rewriting them completely less than
one-tenth of the price he got for his stories), but no''—he
sighed, fading his smile—''no, De Castro was still alive
pestering Lovecraft and visiting him in Providence after
de Castries's death.

"To resume about de Castries; we don't know if his
young Polish mistress accompanied him and possibly was
the mysterious veiled lady who some said turned up at the
same time he did in San Francisco. Ricker thought so.
Klaas was inclined to doubt it. Ricker tended to romance
about the Pole. He pictured her as a brilliant pianist
(they're apt to say that about most Poles, aren't they?
Chopin has much to answer for) who had totally sup-
pressed that talent in order to put all her amazing command of languages and her profound secretarial skills—
and all the solaces of her fierce young body—at the
disposal and in the service of the still younger genius
whom she adored even more devotedly than she had his
adventurer father.''

"What was her name?" Franz asked.

"I could never learn," Byers replied. "Either Klaas
and Ricker had forgotten, or else—more likely—it was
one of the points on which the old boy went secretive on
them. Besides, there's something so satisfying about just
that one phrase 'his father's young Polish mistress'—
what could be more exotic or alluring?—it makes one
think of harpsichords and oceans of lace, champagne, and
pistols! For, under her cool and learned mask, she seethed
with temperament and with temper, too, as Ricker pictured her; so that she'd almost seem to fly apart or on the
verge of it when in her rages, like an explosive rag doll.
The fellahin feared her, thought she was a witch. It was
during those years in Egypt that she began to go veiled,
Ricker said.

"At still other times she'd be incredibly seductive, the
epitome of Continental femininity, initiating de Castries

into the most voluptuous erotic practices and greatly
deepening and broadening his grasp of culture and
art.

"At all events, de Castries had acquired a lot of dark,
satanic charm from somewhere by the time he arrived at
the City by the Golden Gate. He was, I'd guess, quite a bit
like the Satanist Anton La Vey (who kept a more-or-less
tame lion for a while, did you know?), except that he had
no desire for the usual sort of publicity. He was looking,
rather, for an elite of scintillating, freewheeling folk with
a zest for life at its wildest—and if they had a lot of
money, that wouldn't hurt a bit.

"And of course he found them! Promethean (and
Dionysian) Jack London. George Sterling, fantasy poet
and romantic idol, favorite of the wealthy Bohemian Club
set. Their friend, the brilliant defense attorney Earl Rogers, who later defended Clarence Darrow and saved his
career. Ambrose Bierce, a bitter, becaped old eagle of a
man himself with his *Devil's Dictionary* and matchlessly
terse horror tales. The poetess Nora May French. That
mountain lioness of a woman, Charmian London. Ger-
trude Atherton, somewhere close by. And those were only
the more vital ones.

"And of course they fell upon de Castries with delight.
He was just the sort of human curiosity they (and especially Jack London) loved. Mysterious cosmopolitan background, Munchausen anecdotes, weird and alarming sci-
entific theories, a strong anti-industrial and (we'd say)
antiestablishment bias, the apocalyptic touch, the note of
doom, hints of dark powers—he had them all! For quite a
while he was their darling, their favorite guru of the left-
hand path, almost (and I imagine he thought this himself)
their new god. They even bought copies of his new book
and sat still (and drank) while he read from it. Prize
egotists like Bierce put up with him, and London let him
have stage center for a while—he could afford to. And
they were all quite ready to go along (in theory) with his
dream of a utopia in which megapolitan buildings were
forbidden (had been destroyed or somehow tamed) and

paramentality put to benign use, with themselves the
aristocratic elite and he the master spirit over all.

"Of course most of the ladies were quite taken with him
romantically and several, I gather, eager to go to bed with
him and not above taking the initiative in the matter—
these were dramatic and liberated females for their day,
remember—and yet there's no evidence that he had an
affair with any one of them. The opposite, rather. Apparently, when things got to that point, he'd say something
like, 'My dear, there's nothing I'd like better, truly, but I
must tell you that I have a very savage and jealous mistress
who if I so much as dallied with you, would cut my throat
in bed or stab me in my bath (he *was* quite a bit like Marat,
you know, Franz, and grew to be more so in his later
years), besides dashing acid across your lovely cheeks
and lips, my dear, or driving a hatpin into those bewitch-
ing eyes. She's learned beyond measure in the weird, yet a
tigress.'

"He'd really build this (imaginary?) creature up to
them, I'm told, until sometimes it wasn't clear whether it
was a real woman, or a goddess, or some sort of
metaphorical entity that he was talking about. 'She is all
merciless night animal,' he would say, 'yet with a wisdom
that goes back to Egypt and beyond—and which is invalu-
able to me. For she is my spy on buildings, you see, my
intelligencer on metropolitan megastructures. She knows
their secrets and their secret weaknesses, their ponderous
rhythms and dark songs. And she herself is secret as their
shadows. She is my Queen of Night, Our Lady of Darkness.' ''

As Byers dramatized those last words of de Castries,
Franz flashed that Our Lady of Darkness was one of De
Quincy's Ladies of Sorrow, the third and youngest sister,
who always went veiled in black crape. Had de Castries
known that? And was his Queen of Night Mozart's?—all-
powerful save for the magic flute and Papageno's bells?
But Byers continued:

"For you see, Franz, there were these continuing re-
ports, flouted by some, of de Castries being visited or

pestered by a veiled lady who wore flowing dresses and
either a turban or a wide and floppy-brimmed hat, yet was
very swift in her movements. They'd be glimpsed together across a busy street or on the Embarcadero or in a park
or at the other end of a crowded theater lobby, generally
walking rapidly and gesticulating excitedly or angrily at
each other; but when you caught up with him, she would
be gone. Or if, as on a few claimed occasions, she were
still there, he would never introduce her or speak to her or
act in any way as if he knew her. Except he would seem
irritable and—one or two said—frightened.''

"What was *her* name?" Franz pressed.

Byers quirked a smile. "As I just told you, my dear
Franz, he'd never introduce her. At most he'd refer to her
as 'that woman' or sometimes, oddly, 'that headstrong
and pestiferous girl.' Perhaps, despite all his dark charms
and tyrannies and S-M aura, he was afraid of women and
she somehow stood for or embodied that fear.

"Reactions to this mysterious figure varied. The men
tended to be indulgent, intrigued, and speculative, even
wildly so—it was suggested at various times that she was
Isadora Duncan, Eleanora Duse, and Sarah Bernhardt,
though they would have been, respectively, about twenty,
forty, and sixty at that time. But true glamour is ageless,
they say; consider Marlene Dietrich or Arletty, or that
doyenne of them all—Cleopatra. There was always the
disguising black veil, you see, though sometimes it carried an array of black polka dots, like ranked beauty
marks, 'or as if she'd had the black smallpox,' one lady is
said to have said nastily.

"All the women, for that matter, uniformly loathed
her.

"Of course, all this is probably somewhat distorted by
my getting it mostly as filtered through Klaas and Ricker.
Ricker, making a lot of the references to Egyptian wisdom
and learnedness, thought the mystery lady was still the
Polish mistress, gone mad through love, and he was
somewhat critical of de Castries for his treatment of her.

"And of course all this left the way open for endless

speculations about de Castries's sex life. Some said he was a homosexual. Even in those days 'the cool, gray city of love,' as Sterling epitomized it, had its homophiles—'cool, gay city?' Others, that he was very kinky in an S-M way—bondage and discipline of the direst sort. (Quite a few chaps have accidentally strangled themselves that way, you know.) Almost in one breath it was said he was a pederast, a pervert, a fetishist, utterly asexual, or else that only slim little girls could satisfy his Tiberian lusts—I'm sorry if I offend you, Franz, but truly all the lefthand paths and their typical guides or conductresses were mentioned.

"However, all this is really by-the-by. The important consideration is that for a while de Castries seemed to have his chosen group just where he wanted them."

20

DONALDUS CONTINUED. "The high point of Thibaut de Castries's San Francisco adventure came when with much hushhush and weedings out and secret messages and some rare private occult pomps and ceremonies, I suppose, he organized the Hermetic Order—"

"Is that the Hermetic Order that Smith, or the journal, mentions?" Franz interrupted. He had been listening with a mixture of fascination, irritation, and wry amusement, with at least half his attention clearly elsewhere, but he had grown more attentive at mention of the Grand Cipher.

"It is," Byers nodded, "I'll explain. In England at that time there was the Hermetic Order of the Golden Dawn, an occult society with members like the mystic poet Yeats, who talked with vegetables and bees and lakes, and Dion Fortune and George Russell—A.E.—and your beloved Arthur Machen—you know, Franz, I've always thought that in his *The Great God Pan* the sexually sinister *femme fatale* Helen Vaughan was based on the real-life Satanist Diana Vaughan, even though *her* memoirs—and perhaps she herself—were a hoax perpetrated by the French journalist, Gabriel Jogand . . ."

Franz nodded impatiently, restraining his impulse to say, "Get on with it, Donaldus!"

The other got the point. "Well, anyhow," he continued, "in 1898 Aleister Crowley managed to join the Gilded Dayspringers (neat, eh?) and almost broke up the society by his demands for Satanistic rituals, black magic, and other real tough stuff.

"In imitation, but also as a sardonic challenge, de

Castries called *his* society the Hermetic Order of the Onyx
Dusk. He is said to have worn a large black ring of *pietra
dura* work with a bezel of mosaicked onyx, obsidian,
ebony, and black opal polished flat, depicting a predatory
black bird, perhaps a raven.

"It was at this point that things began to go wrong for
de Castries and that the atmosphere became, by degrees,
very nasty. Unfortunately, it's also the period for which
I've had the most difficulty getting information that's at
all reliable—or even any information at all, for reasons
which are, or will become, very obvious.

"As nearly as I can reconstruct it, this is what happened. As soon as his secret society had been constituted,
Thibaut revealed to its double handful of highly select
members that his utopia was not a far-off dream, but an
immediate prospect, and that it was to be achieved by
violent revolution, both material and spiritual (that is,
paramental) and that the chief and at first the sole instrument of that revolution was to be the Hermetic Order of
the Onyx Dusk.

"This violent revolution was to begin with acts of
terrorism somewhat resembling those the Nihilists were
carrying out in Russia at that time (just before the abortive
Revolution of 1905), but with a lot of a new sort of black
magic (his megapolisomancy) thrown in. Demoralization
rather than slaughter was to be the aim, at least at first.
Black-powder bombs were to be set off in public places
and on the roofs of big buildings during the deserted hours
of the night. Other big buildings were to be plunged into
darkness by locating and throwing their main switches.
Anonymous letters and phone calls would heighten the
hysteria.

"But more important would be the megapolisomantic
operations, which would cause 'buildings to crumple to
rubble, people to go screaming mad, until every last soul
is in panic flight from San Francisco, choking the roads
and foundering the ferries'—at least that's what Klaas
said de Castries confided to him many years later while in
a rare communicative mood. Say, Franz, did you know

that Nicola Tesla, America's other electrical wizard, claimed in his last years to have invented or at least envisaged a device small enough to be smuggled into a building in a dispatch case and left there to shake the building to pieces at a preset time by sympathetic vibrations? Herman Klaas told me that too. But I digress.

"These magical or pseudoscientific acts (what would you call them?) would require absolute obedience on the part of Thibaut's assistants—which was the next demand Thibaut seems to have made on every last one of his acolytes in the Hermetic Order of the Onyx Dusk. One of them would be ordered to go to a specific address in San Francisco at a specified time and simply stand there for two hours, blanking his (or her) mind, or else trying to hold one thought. Or he'd be directed to take a bar of copper or a small box of coal or a toy balloon filled with hydrogen to a certain floor in a certain big building and simply leave it there (the balloon against the ceiling), again at a specified time. Apparently the elements were supposed to act as catalysts. Or two or three of them would be commanded to meet in a certain hotel lobby or at a certain park bench and just sit there together without speaking for half an hour. And everyone would be expected to obey every order unquestioningly and unhesitatingly, in exact detail, or else there would be (I suppose) various chilling Carbonari-style penalties and reprisals.

"Big buildings were always the main targets of his megapolisomancy—he claimed they were the chief concentration-points for city-stuff that poisoned great metropolises or weighed them down intolerably. Ten years earlier, according to one story, he had joined other Parisians in opposing the erection of the Eiffel Tower. A professor of mathematics had calculated that the structure would collapse when it reached the height of seven hundred feet, but Thibaut had simply claimed that all that naked steel looking down upon the city from the sky would drive Paris mad. (And considering subsequent events, Franz, I've sometimes thought that a case could be made out that it did just that. World Wars One and Two brought on like locust plagues by overly concentrated populations due to a rash or fever of high buildings—is that so fabulous?) But since he had found he couldn't stop the erection of such buildings, Thibaut had turned to the problem of their control. In some ways, you know, he had the mentality of an animal trainer—inherited from his Africa-traveled father, perhaps?

"Thibaut seems to have thought that there was—or that he had invented—a kind of mathematics whereby minds and big buildings (and paramental entities?) could be manipulated. Neo-Pythagorean metageometry, he called it. It was all a question of knowing the right times and *spots* (he'd quote Archimedes: 'Give me a place to stand and I will move the world') and then conveying there the right person (and mind) or material object. He also seemed to have believed that a limited clairvoyance and clairaudience and prescience existed at certain *places* in mega-cities for certain people. Once he started to outline in detail to Klaas a single act of megapolisomancy—give him the formula for it, so to speak—but then he got suspicious.

"Though there *is* one other anecdote about the megamagic thing, I'm inclined to doubt its authenticity, but it *is* attractive. It seems that Thibaut proposed to give a warning shake to the Hobart Building, or at any rate one of those early flatiron structures on Market—whether it would actually fall down would depend on the integrity of the builder, the old boy's supposed to have said. In this case his four volunteers or conscripts were (improbably?) Jack London, George Sterling, an octoroon ragtime singer named Olive Church, who was a protégée of that old voodoo queen, etcetera, Mammy Pleasant, and a man named Fenner.

"You know Lotta's Fountain there on Market?—gift to the city of Lotta Crabtree, 'the toast of the goldfields,' who was taught dancing (and related arts?) by Lola Montez (she of the spider dance and Ludwig of Bavaria and all). Well, the four acolytes were supposed to approach the fountain by streets that would trace the four arms of a counterclockwise swastika centering on the fountain while concentrating in their mind on the four points of the compass and bearing objects representing the four elements—Olive a potted lily for earth, Fenner a magnum of champagne for fluid, Sterling a rather large toy hydrogen-filled balloon for the gaseous, and Jack a long cigar for fire.

"They were supposed to arrive simultaneously and introduce their burdens into the fountain, George bubbling his hydrogen through its water and Jack extinguishing his cigar in the same.

"Olive and Fenner arrived first, Fenner somewhat drunk—perhaps he had been sampling his offering and we may assume that all four of them were at least somewhat 'elevated.' Well, apparently Fenner had been nursing a lech for Olive and she'd been turning him down, and now he wanted her to drink champagne with him and she wouldn't and he tried to force it on her and succeeded in sloshing it over her bosom *and* the potted lily she was holding and down her dress.

"While they were struggling that way at the fountain's edge, George came up protesting and tried to control Fenner without letting go of his balloon, with Olive shrieking and laughing at them while they were scuffling and while she still hugged the potted lily to her wet breasts.

"At this point Jack came up behind them, drunkest of all, and getting an irresistible inspiration thrust out his cigar at arm's length and touched off the balloon with its glowing tip.

"There was quite a loud, flaming explosion. Eyebrows were singed. Fenner, who thought Sterling had shot him, fell flat on his back in the fountain, letting go the magnum, which shattered on the sidewalk. Olive dropped her pot and went into hysterics. George was livid with fury at Jack, who was laughing like a demented god—while Thibaut was doubtless cursing them blackly from the sidelines somewhere.

"The next day they all discovered that almost exactly at

the same time that night a small brick warehouse behind Rincon Hill had collapsed into a pile of masonry. Age and structural inadequacy were given as the causes, but of course Thibaut claimed it was his mega-magic misfiring because of their general frivolousness and Jack's idiot prank.

"I don't know if there's any truth to that whole story—at best probably distorted in the telling for comedy's sake. Still, it does give an idea, a sort of atmosphere at least.

"Well, in any case you can imagine how those prima donnas that he'd recruited reacted to Thibaut's demands. Conceivably Jack London and George Sterling might have gone through with things like the light-switch business for a lark, if they'd been drunk enough when Thibaut asked them. And even crotchety old Bierce might have enjoyed a little black-powder thunder, if someone else did all the work and set it off. But when he asked them to do *boring* things he wouldn't explain, it was too much. A dashing and eccentric society lady who was a great beauty (and an acolyte) is supposed to have said, "If only he'd asked me to do something *challenging*, such as seduce President Roosevelt (she'd have meant Teddy, Franz) or appear naked in the rotunda of the City of Paris and then swim out to the Seal Rocks and chain myself to them like Andromeda. But just to stand in front of the public library with seven rather large steel ball bearings in my brassiere, thinking of the South Pole and saying nothing for an hour and twenty minutes—I *ask* you, darling!"

"When it got down to cases, you see, they must simply have refused to take him seriously—either his revolution or his new black magic. Jack London was a Marxist socialist from way back and had written his way through a violent class war in his science-fiction novel *The Iron Heel*. He could and would have poked holes in both the theory and the practice of Thibaut's Reign of Terror. And he'd have known that the first city to elect a Union Labor Party government was hardly the place to start a counterrevolution. He also was a Darwinian materialist and knew his science. He'd have been able to show up

Thibaut's 'new black science' as a pseudoscientific travesty and just another name for magic, with all the unexplained action at a distance.

"At any rate, they all refused to help him make even a test-run of his mega-magic. Or perhaps a few of them went along with it once or twice—the Lotta's Fountain sort of thing—and nothing happened.

"I suppose that at this point he lost his temper and began to thunder orders and invoke penalties. And they just laughed at him—and when he wouldn't see that the game was over and kept up with it, simply walked away from him.

"Or taken more active measures. I can imagine someone like London simply picking up the furious, spluttering little man by his coat collar and the seat of his pants and pitching him out."

Byers's eyebrows lifted. "Which reminds me, Franz, that Lovecraft's client De Castro knew Ambrose Bierce and claimed to have collaborated with him, but at their last meeting Bierce sped De Castro's departure by breaking a walking stick over his head. Really quite similar to what I was hypothesizing for de Castries. Such an attractive theory—that they were the same! But no, for De Castro was at Lovecraft to rewrite his memoirs of Bierce after de Castries's death."

He sighed, then recovered swiftly with, "At any rate, something like that could have completed the transformation of Thibaut de Castries from a fascinating freak whom one humored into an unpleasant old bore, troublemaker, borrower, *and blackmailer*, against whom one protected oneself by whatever measures were necessary. Yes, Franz, there's the persistent rumor that he tried to and in some cases did blackmail his former disciples by threatening to reveal scandals he had learned about in the days when they were free with each other, or simply that they had been members of a terrorist organization—his own! Twice at this time he seems to have disappeared completely for several months, very likely because he was serving jail sentences—something several of his ex-acolytes were powerful enough to have managed easily, though I've never been able to track down an instance; so many records were destroyed in the quake.

"But some of the old dark glamour must have lingered about him for quite a while in the eyes of his ex-acolytes— the feeling that he was a being with sinister, paranatural powers—for when the earthquake did come very early in the morning of April eighteenth, 1906, thundering up Market in brick and concrete waves from the west and killing its hundreds, one of his lapsed acolytes, probably recalling his intimations of a magic that would topple skyscrapers, is supposed to have said, 'He's done it! The old devil's done it!'

"And there's the suggestion that Thibaut tried to use the earthquake in his blackmailing—you know, 'I've done it once. I can do it again.' Apparently he'd use anything that occurred to him to try to frighten people. In a couple of instances he's supposed to have threatened people with his Queen of Night, his Lady of Darkness (his old mystery lady or girl)—that if they didn't fork up, he'd send his Black Tigress after them.

"But mostly my information for this period is very sketchy and one-sided. The people who'd known him best were all trying to forget him (suppress him, you might say), while my two chief informants, Klaas and Ricker, knew him only as an old man in the 1920s and had heard only his side (or sides!) of the story. Ricker, who was nonpolitical, thought of him as a great scholar and metaphysician, who had been promised money and support by a group of wealthy, frivolous people and then cruelly disappointed, abandoned. He never seriously believed the revolution part. Klaas did, and viewed de Castries as a failed great rebel, a modern John Brown or Sam Adams or Marat, who'd been betrayed by wealthy, pseudoartistic, thrill-seeking backers who'd then gotten cold feet. They both indignantly rejected the blackmail stories."

Franz interposed, "What about his mystery lady—was

she still around? What did Klaas and Ricker have to say about her?''

Byers shook his head. ''She was completely vanished by the 1920s—if she ever had any real existence in the first place. To Ricker and Klaas she was just one more story—one more of the endlessly fascinating stories they teased out of the old man from time to time. Or else (not so fascinating!) endured in repetition. According to them, he enjoyed no female society whatever while they knew him. Except Klaas once let slip the thought the old man occasionally hired a prostitute—refused to talk about it further when I pressed him, said it was the old man's business, no one else's. While Ricker said the old boy had a sentimental interest in ('a soft spot in his heart for') little girls—all most innocent, a modern Lewis Carroll, he insisted. Both of them vehemently denied any suggestion of a kinky sex life on the old man's part, just as they had denied the blackmail stories and the even nastier rumors that came later on: that de Castries was devoting his declining years to getting revenge on his betrayers by somehow doing them to death or suicide by black magic.''

''I know about some of those cases,'' Franz said, ''at least the ones I imagine you're going to mention. What happened to Nora May French?''

''She was the first to go. In 1907, just a year after the quake. A clear case of suicide. She died most painfully by poison—very tragic.''

''And when did Sterling die?''

''November seventeenth, 1926.''

Franz said thoughtfully, though still not lost in thought, ''There certainly seems to have been a suicidal drive at work, though operating over a period of twenty years. A good case can be made out that it was a death wish drove Bierce to go to Mexico when he did—a war-haunted life, so why not such a death?—and probably attach himself to Pancho Villa's rebels as a sort of unofficial revolution-correspondent and most likely get himself shot as an uppity old gringo who wouldn't stay silent for the devil

himself. While Sterling was known to have carried a vial
of cyanide in his vest pocket for years, whether he finally
took it by accident (pretty far-fetched) or by intention.
And then there was that time (Rogers's daughter tells
about it in her book) when Jack London disappeared on a
five-day spree and then came home when Charmian and
Rogers's daughter and several other worried people were
gathered, and with the mischievous, icy logic of a man
who'd drunk himself sober, challenged George Sterling
and Rogers *not to sit up with the corpse*. Though I'd think
alcohol was enough villain there, without bringing in any
of de Castries's black magic, or its power of suggestion.''

"What'd London mean by that?" Byers asked, squint-
ing as he carefully measured out for himself more brandy.

"That when they felt life losing its zest, their powers
starting to fail, they take the Noseless One by the arm
without waiting to be asked, and exit laughing.''

"The Noseless One?''

"Why, simply, London's sobriquet for Death himself—the skull beneath the skin. The nose is all cartilage
and so the skull—''

Byers's eyes widened and he suddenly shot a finger
toward his guest.

"Franz!'' he asked excitedly. "That paramental you
saw—wasn't it noseless?''

As if he'd just received a posthypnotic command,
Franz's eyes shut tight, he jerked back his face a little, and
started to throw his hands in front of it. Byers' words had
brought the pale brown, blank, triangular muzzle vividly
back to his mind's eye.

"Don't''—he said carefully—"say things like that
again without warning. Yes, it was noseless.''

"My dear Franz, I will not. Please excuse me. I did not
fully realize until now what effect the sight of it must have
upon a person.''

"All right, all right,'' Franz said quietly. "So four
acolytes died somewhat ahead of their time (except
perhaps for Bierce), victims of their rampant
psyches . . . or of something else.''

"And at least an equal number of less prominent acolytes," Byers took up again quite smoothly. "You know,
Franz, I've always been impressed by how in London's
last great novel, *The Star Rover*, mind triumphs completely over matter. By frightfully intense self-discipline,
a lifer at San Quentin is enabled to escape in spirit through
the thick walls of his prison house and move at will
through the world and relive his past reincarnations, redie
his deaths. Somehow that makes me think of old de
Castries in the 1920s, living alone in downtown cheap
hotels and brooding, brooding, brooding about past hopes
and glories and disasters. And (dreaming meanwhile of
foul, unending tortures) about the wrongs done him and
about revenge (whether or not he actually worked something there) and about . . . who knows what else? Sending
his mind upon . . . who knows what journeys?"

21

"AND NOW," Byers said, dropping his voice, "I must tell you of Thibaut de Castries's last acolyte and final end. Remember that during this period we must picture him as a bent old man, taciturn most of the time, always depressed, and getting paranoid. For instance, now, he had a thing about never touching metal surfaces and fixtures, because his enemies were trying to electrocute him. Sometimes he was afraid they were poisoning his tap water in the pipes. He seldom would go out, for fear a car would jump the curb and get him, and he was no longer spry enough to dodge, or an enemy would shatter his skull with a brick or tile dropped from a high roof. At the same time he was frequently changing his hotel, to throw them off his trail. Now his only contacts with former associates were his dogged attempts to get back and burn all copies of his book, though there may still have been some blackmailing and plain begging. Ricker and Klaas witnessed one such book burning. Grotesque affair!—he burned two copies in his bathtub. They remembered opening the windows and fanning out the smoke. With one or two exceptions, they were his only visitors—lonely and eccentric types themselves, and already failed men like himself although they were only in their thirties at the time.

"Then Clark Ashton Smith came—the same age, but brimming with poetry and imagination and creative energy. Clark had been hard hit by George Sterling's nasty death and had felt driven to look up such friends and acquaintances of his poetic mentor as he could find. De

Castries felt old fires stir. Here was another of the brilliant, vital ones he'd always sought. He was tempted (finally yielding entirely) to exert his formidable charm for a last time, to tell his fabulous tales, to expound compellingly his eerie theories, and to weave his spells.

"And Clark Ashton, a lover of the weird and of its beauty, highly intelligent, yet in some ways still a naive small-town youth, emotionally turbulent, made a most gratifying audience. For several weeks Clark delayed his return to Auburn, fearfully reveling in the ominous, wonder-shot, strangely *real* world that old Tiberius, the scarecrow emperor of terror and mysteries, painted for him afresh each day—a San Francisco of spectral though rock-solid megabuildings and invisible paramental entities more real than life. It's easy to see why the Tiberius metaphor caught Clark's fancy. At one point he wrote—hold on for a moment, Franz, while I get that photocopy—"

"There's no need," Franz said, dragging the journal itself out of his side pocket. The binoculars came out with it and dropped to the thickly carpeted floor with a shivery little clash of the broken glass inside.

Byers's eyes followed them with morbid curiosity. "So those are the glasses that (Take warning, Franz!) several times saw a paramental entity and were in the end destroyed by it." His gaze shifted to the journal. "Franz, you sly dog! You came prepared for at least part of this discussion before you ever went to Corona Heights today!"

Franz picked up the binoculars and put them on the low table beside his overflowing ashtray, meanwhile glancing rapidly around the room and at its windows, where the gold had darkened a little. He said quietly, "It seems to me, Donaldus, you've been holding out, too. You take for granted now that Smith wrote the journal, but in the Haight and even in the letters we exchanged afterwards, you said you were uncertain."

"You've got me," Byers admitted with a rather odd little smile, perhaps ashamed. "But it really seemed *wise*, Franz, to let as few people in on it as possible. Now of course you know as much as I do, or will in a few minutes, but . . . The most camp of clichés is 'There are some things man was not meant to know,' but there are times when I believe it really applies to Thibaut de Castries and the paranatural. Might I see the journal?''

Franz flipped it across. Byers caught it as if it were made of eggshell, and with an aggrieved look at his guest carefully opened it and as carefully turned a couple of pages. ''Yes, here it is. 'Three hours today at 607 Rhodes. What a locus for genius! How prosaick?—as Howard would spell it. And yet Tiberius is Tiberius indeed, miserly doling out his dark Thrasyllus-secrets in this canyoned, cavernous Capri called San Francisco to his frightened young heir (God, no! Not I!) Caligula. And wondering how soon I, too, will go mad.' ''

As he finished reading aloud, Byers began to turn the next pages, one at a time, and kept it up even when he came to the blank ones. Now and then he'd look up at Franz, but he examined each page minutely with fingers and eyes before he turned it.

He said conversationally, ''Clark did think of San Francisco as a modern Rome, you know, both cities with their seven hills. From Auburn he'd seen George Sterling and the rest living as if all life were a Roman holiday. With Carmel perhaps analogous to Capri, which was simply Tiberius's Little Rome, for the more advanced fun and games. Fishermen brought fresh-caught lobsters to the goatish old emperor; Sterling dove for giant abalone with his knife. Of course, Rhodes was the Capri of Tiberius's early middle years. No, I can see why Clark would not have wanted to be Caligula. 'Art, like the bartender, is never drunk'—or really schiz. Hello, what's this?''

His fingernails were gently teasing at the edge of a page. ''It's clear you're not a bibliophile, dear Franz. I should have gone ahead and stolen the book from you that evening in the Haight, as at one point I fully intended to, except that something gallant in your drunken manner touched my conscience, which is *never* a good guide to follow. There!''

With the ghostliest of cracklings the page came apart into two, revealing writing hidden between.

He reported, "It's black as new—India ink, for certain—but done very lightly so as not to groove the paper in the slightest. Then a few tiny drops of gum arabic, not enough to wrinkle, and hey presto!—it's hidden quite neatly. The obscurity of the obvious. 'Upon their vestments is a writing no man may see . . .' *Oh dear me, no!*"

He resolutely averted his eyes, which had been reading while he spoke. Then he stood up and holding the journal at arm's length came over and squatted on his hams, so close beside Franz that his brandy breath was obvious, and held the newly liberated page spread before their faces. Only the right-hand one was written upon, in very black yet spider-fine characters very neatly drawn and not remotely like Smith's handwriting.

"Thank you," Franz said. "This is weird. I riffled through those pages a dozen times."

"But you did not examine each one minutely with the true bibliophile's profound mistrust. The signatory initials indicate it was written by old Tiberius himself. And I'm sharing this with you not so much out of courtesy, as fear. Glancing at the opening, I got the feeling this was something I did not want to read all by myself. This way feels safer—at least it spread the danger."

Together they silently read the following:

A CURSE upon Master Clark Ashton Smith and all his heirs, who thought to pick my brain and slip away, false fleeting agent of my old enemies. Upon him the Long Death, the paramental agony! when he strays back as all men do. The fulcrum (0) and the Cipher (A) shall be here, at his *beloved* 607 Rhodes. I'll be at rest in my appointed spot (1) under the Bishop's Seat, the heaviest ashes that he ever felt. Then when the weights are on at Sutro Mount (4) and Monkey Clay (5) [(4) + (1) = (5)] *BE his Life Squeezed Away*. Committed to Cipher in my 50-Book (A). Go out, my little book (B) into the world,

and lie in wait in stalls and lurk on shelves for the
unwary purchaser. Go out, my little book, and break
some necks!

                                        TdC

As he finished reading it, Franz's mind was whirling
with so many names of places and things both familiar and
strange that he had to prod himself to remind himself to
check visually the windows and doors and corners of
Byers's gorgeous living room, now filling with shadows.
That business about "when the weights are on"—he
couldn't imagine what it meant, but taken together with
"heaviest ashes," it made him think of the old man
pressed to death with heavy stones on a plank on his chest
for refusing to testify at the Salem witchcraft trial of 1692,
as if a confession could be forced out like a last breath.

"Monkey Clay," Byers muttered puzzledly. "Ape of
clay? Poor suffering Man, molded of dust?"

Franz shook his head. And in the midst of all, he
thought, that damnably puzzling 607 Rhodes! which kept
turning up again and again, and had in a way touched all
this off.

And to think he'd had this book for years and not
spotted the secret. It made a person suspect and distrust all
things closest to him, his most familiar possessions. What
might not be hidden inside the lining of your clothes, or in
your right-hand trousers pocket (or for a woman, in her
handbag or bra), or in the cake of soap with which you
washed (which might have a razor blade inside).

Also to think that he was looking at last at de Castries's
own handwriting, so neatly drawn and yet so crabbed for
all that.

One detail puzzled him differently. "Donaldus," he
said, "how would de Castries ever have got hold of
Smith's journal?"

Byers let out a long alcohol-laden sigh, massaged his
face with his hands (Franz clutched the journal to keep it
from falling), and said, "Oh, that. Klaas and Ricker both
told me that de Castries was quite worried and hurt when

Clark went back to Auburn (it turned out) without warning, after visiting the old man every day for a month or so.
De Castries was so bothered, they said, that he went over
to Clark's cheap roominghouse and convinced them he
was Clark's uncle, so that they gave him some things
Clark had left behind when he'd checked out in a great
tearing hurry. 'I'll keep them for little Clark,' he told
Klaas and Ricker and then later (after they'd heard from
Clark) he added, 'I've shipped him back his things.' They
never suspected that the old man ever entertained any hard
feelings about Clark.''

Franz nodded. ''But then how did the journal (now with
the curse in it) get from de Castries to wherever I bought
it?''

Byers said wearily, ''Who knows? The curse, though,
does remind me of another side of de Castries's character
that I haven't mentioned: his fondness for rather cruel
practical jokes. Despite his morbid fear of electricity, he
had a chair Ricker helped rig for him to give the sitter an
electric shock through the cushion that he kept for sales-
men and salesladies, children, and other stray visitors. He
nearly got into police trouble through that too. Some
young lady looking for typing work got her bottom
burned. Come to think of it, that has an S-M feeling, don't
you think?—the genuine sadomasochistic touch. Electricity—bringer of thrills and pain. Don't writers speak of
electric kisses? Ah, the evil that lurks in the hearts of
men,'' Byers finished sententiously and stood up, leaving
the journal in Franz's hands, and went back to his place.
Franz looked at him questioningly, holding out the journal
toward him a little, but his host said, pouring himself
more brandy, ''No, you keep it. It's yours. After all, you
were—are—the purchaser. Only for Heaven's sake take
better care of it! It's a *very* rare item.''

''But what do you think of it, Donaldus?'' Franz asked.

Donaldus shrugged as he began to sip. ''A shivery
document indeed,'' he said, smiling at Franz as if he were
very glad the latter had it. ''And it really did lie in wait in
stalls and lurk on shelves for many years, apparently.

Franz, don't you recall *anything* about where you bought
it?''

"I've tried and tried," Franz said tormentedly. "The
place was in the Haight, I'm fairly sure of that.
Called . . . the In Group? The Black Spot? The Black
Dog? The Grey Cockatoo? No, none of those, and I've
tried hundreds of names. I think that 'black' was in it, but I
believe the proprietor was a white man. And there was a
little girl—maybe his daughter—helping him. Not so
little, really—she was into puberty, I seem to recall, and
well aware of it. Pushing herself at me—all this is very
vague. I also seem to recall (I was drunk of course) being
attracted to her," he confessed somewhat ashamedly.

"My dear Franz, aren't we all?" Byers observed.
"The little darlings, barely kissed by sex, but don't they
know it! Who can resist? Do you recall what you paid for
the books?''

"Something pretty high, I think. But now I'm beginning to guess and imagine.''

"You could search through the Haight, street by street,
of course.''

"I suppose I could, if it's still there and hasn't changed
its name. Why don't you get on with your story,
Donaldus?''

"Very well. There's not much more of it. You know,
Franz, there's one indication that that . . . er . . . curse
isn't particularly efficacious. Clark lived a long and pro-
ductive life, thirty-three more years. Reassuring, don't
you think?''

"He didn't stray back to San Francisco," Franz said
shortly. "At least not very often.''

"That's true. Well, after Clark left, de Castries re-
mained . . . just a lonely and gloomy old man. He once
told George Ricker at about this time a very unromantic
story of his past: that he was French-Canadian and had
grown up in northern Vermont, his father by turns a small-
town printer and a farmer, always a failure, and he a
lonely and unhappy child. It has the ring of truth, don't
you think? And it makes one wonder what the sex life of

such a person would have been. No mistresses at all, I'd say, let alone intellectual, mysterious, and foreign ones. Well, anyhow, now he'd had his last fling (with Clark) at playing the omnipotent sinister sorcerer, and it had turned out as bitterly as it had the first time in *fin de siècle* San Francisco (if that was the first). Gloomy and lonely. He had only one other literary acquaintance at that time—or friend of any sort, for that matter. Klaas and Ricker both vouch for it. Dashiell Hammett, who was living in San Francisco in an apartment at Post and Hyde, and writing *The Maltese Falcon.* Those bookstore names you were trying out reminded me of it—the Black Dog and a cockatoo. You see, the fabulously jeweled gold falcon enameled black (and finally proven a fake) is sometimes called the Black Bird in Hammett's detective story. He and de Castries talked a lot about black treasures, Klaas and Ricker told me. And about the historical background of Hammett's book—the Knights Hospitalers (later of Malta) who created the falcon and how they'd once been the Knights of Rhodes—''

"Rhodes turning up again!" Franz interjected. "That damn 607 Rhodes!"

"Yes," Byers agreed. "First Tiberius, then the Hospitalers. They held the island for two hundred years and were finally driven out of it by the sultan Sulayman I in 1522. But about the Black Bird—you'll recall what I told you of de Castries's *pietra dura* ring of mosaicked black semiprecious stuff depicting a black bird? Klaas claimed it was the inspiration for *The Maltese Falcon!* One needn't go that far, of course, but just the same it's all very odd indeed, don't you think? De Castries and Hammett. The black magician and the tough detective."

"Not so odd as all that when you think about it," Franz countered, his eyes on one of their roving trips again. "Besides being one of America's few great novelists, Hammett was a rather lonely and taciturn man himself, with an almost fabulous integrity. He elected to serve a sentence in a federal prison rather than betray a trust. And he enlisted in World War II when he didn't have to and

served it out in the cold Aleutians and finally toughed out
a long last illness. No, he'd have been interested in a queer
old duck like de Castries and showed a hard, unsentimen-
tal compassion toward his loneliness and bitterness and
failures. Go on, Donaldus.''

"There's really nothing more,'' Donaldus said, but his
eyes were flashing. "De Castries died of a coronary
occlusion in 1929 after two weeks in the City Hospital. It
happened in the summertime—I remember Klaas saying
the old man didn't even live to see the stock market crash
and the beginnings of the Great Depression, 'which would
have been a comfort to him because it would have confirmed his theories that because of the self-abuse of mega-
cities, the world was going to hell in a handbasket.'

"So that was that. De Castries was cremated, as he'd
wished, which took his last cash. Ricker and Klaas split
his few possessions. There were of course no relatives.''

"I'm glad of that,'' Franz said. "I mean, that he was
cremated. Oh, I know he died—had to be dead after all
these years—but just the same, along with all the rest
today, I've had this picture of de Castries, a very old man,
but wiry and somehow very fast, still slipping around San
Francisco. Hearing that he not only died in a hospital but
was cremated makes his death more final.''

"In a way,'' Byers agreed, giving him an odd look.
"Klaas had the ashes sitting just inside his front door for a
while in a cheap canister the crematory had furnished,
until he and Ricker figured out what to do with them. They
finally decided to follow de Castries's wish there too,
although it meant an illegal burial and doing it all secretly
at night. Ricker carried a post-digger packaged in newspaper, and Klaas a small spade, similarly wrapped.

"There were two other persons in the funeral party.
Dashiell Hammett—he decided a question for them, as it
happened. They'd been arguing as to whether de Castries's black ring (Klaas had it) should be buried with the
ashes, so they put it up to Hammet, and he said, 'Of
course.' ''

"That figures," Franz said, nodding. "But how very strange."

"Yes, wasn't it?" Byers agreed. "They bound it to the neck of the canister with heavy copper wire. The fourth person—he even carried the ashes—was Clark. I thought that would surprise you. They'd got in touch with him in Auburn and he'd come back just for that night. It shows, come to think of it, that Clark couldn't have known about the curse—or does it? Anyhow, the little burial detail set forth from Klaas's place just after dark. It was a clear night and the moon was gibbous, a few days before full—which was a good thing, as they had some climbing to do where there were no street lights."

"Just the four of them, eh?" Franz prompted when Byers paused.

"Odd you should ask that," Byers said. "After it was all over, Hammett asked Ricker, 'Who the devil was that woman who stayed in the background?—some old flame of his? I expected her to drop out when we got to the rocks, or else join us, but she kept her distance all the way.' It gave Ricker quite a turn—for he, as it happened, hadn't glimpsed anyone. Nor had Klaas or Smith. But Hammett stuck to his story."

Byers looked at Franz with a sort of relish and finished rapidly. "The burial went off without a hitch, though they needed the post-digger—the ground was hard. The only think lacking was the TV tower—that fantastic cross between a dressmaker's dummy and a Burmese pagoda in a feast of red lanterns—to lean down through the night and give a cryptic blessing. The spot was just below a natural rock seat that de Castries had called the Bishop's Seat after the one in Poe's 'Gold Bug' story, and just at the base of that big rock outcropping that is the summit of Corona Heights. Oh, incidentally, another of his whims they gratified—he was burned wearing a bathrobe he'd worn to tatters—a pale old brown one with a cowl."

22

Franz's eyes, engaged in one of their roving all-inspections, got the command to check the glooms and shadows not only for a pale, blank, triangular face with restless snout, but also for the thin, hawkish, ghostly one, tormented and tormenting, murder-bent, of a hyperactive old man looking like something out of Doré's illustrations of Dante's *Inferno*. Since he'd never seen a photograph of de Castries, if any existed, that would have to do.

His mind was busy assimilating the thought that Corona Heights was literally impregnated with Thibaut de Castries. That both yesterday and today he had occupied for rather long periods of time what must almost certainly be the Bishop's Seat of the curse, while only a few yards below in the hard ground were the essential dusts (salts?) and the black ring. How did that go in the cipher in Poe's tale? "Take a good glass in the Bishop's Seat . . ." His glasses were broken, but then he hardly needed them for this short-range work. Which were worse—ghosts or paramentals?—or were they, conceivably, the same? When one was simply on watch for the approach of both or either, that was a rather academic question, no matter how many interesting problems it posed about different levels of reality. Somewhere, deep down, he was aware of being angry, or perhaps only argumentative.

"Turn on some lights, Donaldus," he said in a flat voice.

"I must say you're taking it very coolly," his host said in slightly aggrieved, slightly awed tones.

"What do you expect me to do, panic? Run out in the

street and get shot?—or crushed by falling walls? or cut
by flying glass? I suppose, Donaldus, that you delayed
revealing the exact location of de Castries's grave so that
it would have a greater dramatic impact, and so be truer,
in line with your theory of the identity of reality and art?''

"Exactly! You *do* understand, and I *did* tell you there
would be a ghost and how appropriately the astrological
graffiti served as Thibaut's epitaph, or tomb decor. But
isn't it all so very *amazing*, Franz? To think that when you
first looked from your window at Corona Heights,
Thibaut de Castries's mortal remains unknown to you—''

"Turn on some lights," Franz repeated. "What I find
amazing, Donaldus, is that you've known about paramental entities for many years, and about the highly sinister
activities of de Castries and the suggestive circumstances
of his burial, and yet take no more precautions against
them than you do. You're like a soldier dancing the light
fantastic in no-man's-land. Always remembering that I,
or you, or both of us may at this moment be totally insane.
Of course, you learned about the curse only just now, if I
can trust you. And you did bolt the door after I came in.
Turn on some lights!''

Byers complied at last. A dull gold refulgence streamed
from the large globular shade suspended above them. He
moved to the front hall, somewhat reluctantly, it appeared, and flicked a switch, then to the back of the living
room, where he did the same and then busied himself
opening another bottle of brandy. The windows became
dark rectangles netted with gold. Full night had fallen.
But at least the shadows inside had been banished.

All this while he was saying in a voice that had grown
rather listless and dispirited now that his tale had been
told, "Of course you can trust me, Franz. It was out of
consideration for your own safety that I didn't tell you
about de Castries. Until today, when it became clear you
were into the business, like it or not. I don't go babbling
about it all, believe me. If I've learned one thing over the
years, it's that it's a mercy *not* to tell anyone about the
darker side of de Castries and his theories. That's why

I've never even *considered* publishing a monograph about the man. What other reason could I have for that?—such a book would be brilliant. Fa Lo Suee knows all—one can't hide anything from a serious lover—but she has a very strong mind, as I've suggested. In fact, after you called this morning, I suggested to her as she was going out that if she had some spare time she have another look for the bookstore where you bought the journal—she has a talent for such problems. She smiled and said that, as it happened, she'd been planning to do just that.

"Also," he went on, "you say I take no precautions against them, but I do, I do! According to Klaas and Ricker the old man once mentioned three protections against 'undesirable influences': *silver*, old antidote to werewolfry (another reason I've encouraged Fa Lo Suee in her art), *abstract designs*, those old attention-trappers (hopefully the attention of paramentals too—hence all the mazelike arabesques you see about you), and *stars*, the primal pentagram—it was I, going there on several cold dawns, when I'd be sure of privacy, who sprayed most of those astrologic graffiti on Corona Heights!"

"Donaldus," Franz said sharply, "you've been a lot deeper and more steadily into this all along than you've told me—and your girlfriend too, apparently."

"Companion," Byers corrected. "Or, if you will, lover. Yes, that's right—it's been one of my chief secondary concerns (primary now) for quite a few years. But what was I saying? Oh, yes, that Fa Lo Suee knows all. So did a couple of her predecessors—a famous interior decorator and a tennis star who was also an actor. Clark, Klaas and Ricker knew—they were my source—but they're all dead. So you see I do try to shield others—and myself up to a point. I regard paramental entities as very real and present dangers, about midway in nature between the atomic bomb and the archetypes of the collective unconscious, which include several highly dangerous characters, as you know. Or between a Charles Manson or Zodiac killer and kappa phenomena as defined by Meleta Denning in *Gnostica*. Or between muggers and elementals, or hepatitis viruses and incubi. They're all of them things any sane man is on guard against.

"But mark this, Franz," he emphasized, pouring out brandy, "despite all my previous knowledge, so much more extensive and of such longer standing than your own, I've never actually *seen* a paramental entity. You have the advantage of me there. And it seems to be *quite* an advantage." And he looked at Franz with a mixture of avidity and dread.

Franz stood up. "Perhaps it is," he said shortly, "at least in making a person stay on guard. You say you're trying to protect yourself, but you don't act that way. Right now—excuse me, Donaldus—you're getting so drunk that you'd be helpless if a paramental entity—"

Byers's eyebrows went up. "You think you could defend yourself against them, resist them, fight them, destroy them, once they're around?" he asked incredulously, his voice strengthening. "Can you stop an atomic missile headed for San Francisco at this moment through the ionosphere? Can you command the germs of cholera? Can you abolish your Anima or your Shadow? Can you say to the poltergeist, 'Don't knock'? or to the Queen of the Night, 'Stay outside?' You can't stand guard twenty-four hours a day for months, for years. Belieye me, I know. A soldier crouched in a dugout can't try to figure out if the next shell will be a direct hit or not. He'd go crazy if he tried. No, Franz, all you can do is to lock the doors and windows, turn on all the lights, and hope they pass you by. And try to forget them. Eat, drink and be merry. Recreate yourself. Here, have a drink."

He came toward Franz carrying in each hand a glass half-full of brandy.

"No, thank you," Franz said harshly, jamming the journal into his coat pocket, to Byers's fleeting distress. Then he picked up the tinkling binoculars and jammed them in the other side pocket, thinking in a flash of the binoculars in James's ghost story "A View from a Hill" that had been magicked to see the past by being filled with a black fluid from boiled bones that had oozed out nastily when they were broken. Could his own binoculars have been somehow doctored or gimmicked so that they saw things that weren't there? A wildly farfetched notion, and anyhow his own binoculars were broken, too.

"I'm sorry, Donaldus, but I've got to go," he said, heading for the hall. He knew that if he stayed he *would* take a drink, starting the old cycle, and the idea of becoming unconscious *and incapable of being roused* was very repellent.

Byers hurried after him. His haste and his gyrations to keep the brandy from spilling would have been comic under other circumstances and if he hadn't been saying in a horrified, plaintive, pleading voice, "You can't go out, it's dark. You can't go out with that old devil or his paramental slipping around. Here, have a drink and stay the night. At least stay for the party. If you're going to stand on guard, you're going to need some rest and recreation. I'm sure you'll find an agreeable and pleasing partner—they'll all be swingers, but intelligent. And if you're afraid of liquor dulling your mind, I've got some cocaine, the purest crystal." He drained one glass and set it down on the hall table. "Look, Franz, I'm frightened, too—and you've been pale ever since I told you where the old devil's dust is laid. Stay for the party. And have just one drink—enough to relax a little. In the end, there's no other way, believe me. You'd just get too tired, trying to watch forever." He swayed a little, wheedling, smiling his pleasantest.

A weight of weariness descended on Franz. He reached toward the glass, but just as he touched it he jerked his fingers away as if they'd been burned.

"Shh," he cautioned as Byers started to speak and he warningly gripped him by the elbow.

In the silence they heard a tiny, faintly grating, sliding metallic sound ending in a soft snap, as of a key being rotated in a lock. Their eyes went to the front door. They saw the brass inner knob revolve.

"It's Fa Lo Suee," Byers said. "I'll have to unbolt the door." He moved to do so.

"Wait!" Franz whispered urgently. "Listen!"

They heard a steady scratching sound that didn't end, as if some intelligent beast was drawing a horny claw round and round on the other side of the painted wood. There rose unbidden in Franz's imagination the paralyzing image of a large black panther crouched close against the other side of the gold-traced white opacity, a green-eyed, gleamingly black panther that was beginning to metamorphose into something more terrible.

"Up to her tricks," Byers muttered and drew the bolt before Franz could move to hinder him.

The door pressed halfway open, and around it came two pale gray, triangular flat feline faces that flittered at the edges and were screeching "Aiii-eee!" it sounded.

Both men recoiled, Franz flinching aside with eyes involuntarily slitted from two pale gray gleaming shapes, a taller and a slenderer one, that whirled past him as they shot menacingly at Byers, who was bent half double in his retreat, one arm thrown shieldingly across his eyes, the other across his groin, while the gleaming wineglass and the small sheet of amber fluid it had contained still sailed through the air from the point where his hand had abandoned them.

Incongruously, Franz's mind registered the odors of brandy, burnt hemp, and a spicy perfume.

The gray shapes converged on Byers, clutching at his groin, and as he gasped and gabbled inarticulately, weakly trying to fend them off, the taller was saying in a husky contralto voice with great enjoyment, "In China, Mr. Nayland Smith, we have ways to make men talk."

Then the brandy was on the pale green wallpaper, the unbroken wineglass on the golden-brown carpet, and the stoned, handsome Chinese woman and equally mind-blown urchin-faced girl had snatched off their gray cat-masks, though laughing wildly and continuing to grope and tickle Byers vigorously, and Franz realized they had both been screeching "Jaime," his host's first name, at the top of their voices.

His extreme fear had left Franz, but not its paralysis.

The latter extended to his vocal cords, so that from the moment of the strange eruption of the two gray-clad females to the moment when he left the house on Beaver Street he never spoke a word but only stood beside the dark rectangle of the open door and observed the busy tableau farther down the hall with a rather cold detachment.

Fa Lo Suee had a spare, somewhat angular figure, a flat face with strong, bony structure, dark eyes that were paradoxically both bright and dull with marijuana (and whatever) and straight dull black hair. Her dark red lips were thin. She wore silver-gray stockings and gloves and a closely fitting dress (of ribbed silver-gray silk) and of the Chinese sort that always looks modern. Her left hand threatened Byers in his midst, her right lay loosely low around the slender waist of her companion.

The latter was a head shorter, almost but not quite skinny, and had sexy little breasts. Her face was actually catlike: receding chin, pouty lips, a snub nose, protuberant blue eyes and low forehead, from which straight blonde hair fell to one side. She looked about seventeen, bratty and worldly wise. She plinked a note in Franz's memory. She wore a pale gray leotard, silver-gray gloves, and a gray cloak of some light material that now hung to one side like her hair. Both of her hands mischievously groped Byers. She had a pink ear and a vicious giggle.

The two cat-masks, cast on the hall table now, were edged with silver sequins and had a few stiff whiskers, but they retained the nasty triangular snouty appearance which had been so unnerving coming around the door.

Donaldus (or Jaime) spoke no really intelligible word himself during this period before Franz's departure, except perhaps "Don't!" but he gasped and squealed and babbled a lot, with breathless little laughs thrown in. He stayed bent half-double and twisting from side to side, his hands constantly but rather ineffectually fending off the clutching ones. His pale violet dressing gown, unbelted, swished as he twisted.

It was the women who did all the talking and at first

only Fa Lo Suee. "We reallly scared you, didn't we?"
she said rapidly. "Jaime scares easily, Shirl, especially
when he's drunk. That was my key scratching the door.
Go on, Shirl, give it to him!" Then resuming her Fu
Manchu voice, "What have you and Dr. Petrie there been
up to? In Honan, Mr. Nayland Smith, we have an infal-
lible Chinese test for homophilia. Or is it possible you're
AC-DC? We have the ancient wisdom of the East, all the
dark lore that Mao Tse-tung's forgotten. Combined with
western science, it's devastating. (That's it, girl, hurt
him!) Remember my thugs and dacoits, Mr. Smith, my
golden scorpions and red six-inch centipedes, my black
spiders with diamond eyes that wait in the dark, then leap!
How would you like one of those dropped down your
pants? Repeat—what have you and Dr. Petrie been doing? Be careful what you say. My assistant, Miss Shirley
Soames (Keep it up, Shirl!) has a rat-trap memory. No lie
will go unnoticed."

Franz, frozen, felt rather as if he were watching cray-
fish and sea anemones scuttling and grasping, fronds
questing, pincers and flower-mouths opening and closing, in a rock pool. The endless play of life.

"Oh, by the way, Jaime, I've solved the problem of the
Smith journal," Fa Lo Suee said in a bright casual voice
while her own hands became more active. "This is Shirl
Soames, Jaime (you're getting to him, girl!), who for
years and years has been her father's assistant at the
Gray's Inn bookstore in the Haight. And she remembers
the whole transaction, although it was four years ago,
because she has a *rat-trap* memory."

The name "Gray's Inn" lit up like neon in Franz's
mind. How had he kept missing it?

"Oh, traps distress you, do they, Nayland Smith?" Fa
Lo Suee went on. "They're cruel to animals, are they?
Western sentimentality! I will have you know, for your
information, that Shirl Soames here can *bite*, as well as
nip exquisitely."

As she was saying that, she was sliding her silk-gloved
right hand down the girl's rump and inward, until the tip

of her middle finger appeared to be resting on the spot
midway between the outer orifices of the reproductive and
digestive systems. The girl appreciatively jogged her hips
from side to side through a very short arc.

Franz took coldly clinical note of those actions and of
the inward fact that under other circumstances it would
have been an exciting gesture, making him want to do so
himself to Shirley Soames, and so be done by. But why
her in particular? Memories stirred.

Fa Lo Suee noticed Franz and turned her head. Giving
him a very civilized glassy-eyed smile, she said politely,
"Ah, you must be Franz Westen, the writer, who phoned
Jaime this morning. So you as well as he will be interested
in what Shirley has to say.

"Shirl, leave off excruciating Jaime. He's had enough
punishment. Is this the gentleman?" And without remov-
ing her hand she gently swung the girl around until she
faced Franz.

Behind them Byers, still bent over, was taking deep
breaths mixed with dying chuckles as he began to recover
from the working over he'd been given.

With amphetamine-bright eyes the girl looked Franz up
and down. While he was realizing that he knew that
feline, foxy little face (face of a cat, presently licking
cream), though on a body skinnier still and another head
shorter.

"That's him, all right," she said in a rapid, sharp voice
that still had something of a brat's "yah! yah!" in it.
"Correct, mister? Four years ago, you bought two old
books tied together out of a lot that had been around for
years that my father'd bought that belonged to a George
Ricker. You were squiffed, really skew-iffed! We were
together in the stacks and I touched you and you looked so
queer. You paid twenty-five dollars for those old books. I
thought you thought you were paying for a chance to feel
me up. Were you? So many of the older men wanted to."
She read something in Franz's expression, her eyes
brightened, and she gave a hoarse little laugh. "No, I got
it! You paid all that money because you were feeling

guilty because you were so drunk you thought—what a laugh!—you'd been molesting me, whereas in my sweet girlish way, I'd been molesting you! I was very good at molesting, it was the first thing dear Daddy taught me. I learnt on him. And I was Daddy's star attraction at the store, and didn't he know it! But I'd already found out girls were nicer.''

All this while she'd continued to jog her little hips lasciviously, leaning back a little, and now she slipped her own right hand behind her, presumably to rest it on Fa Lo Suee's.

Franz looked at Shirley Soames and at the two others, and he knew that all that she had said was true, and he also knew that this was how Jaime Donaldus Byers escaped from his fears (and Fa Lo Suee from hers?). And without a word or any change in his rather stupid expression he turned and walked out the open door.

He had a sharp pang—''I am abandoning Donaldus!''—and two fleeting thoughts—''Shirl Soames and her touchings were the dark, musty, tendriled memory I had on the stairs yesterday morning'' and ''Would Fa Lo Suee immortalize the exquisite moment in slim silver, perhaps titling it 'The Loving Goose'?—but nothing made him pause or reconsider. As he started down the steps, light from the doorway spilling around him, his eyes were already systematically checking the darkness ahead for hostile presences—each corner, each yawning areaway, each shadowy rooftop, each coign of vantage. As he reached the street, the soft light around him vanished as the door behind him was silently shut. That relieved him—it made him less of a target in the full onyx dusk that had now closed once more on San Francisco.

23

As Franz moved cautiously down Beaver Street, his eyes checking the glooms between the rather few lights, he thought of how de Castries had ceased to be a mere parochial devil haunting the lonely hump of Corona Heights (and Franz's own room at 811 Geary?), but a ubiquitous demon, ghost, or paramental inhabiting the whole city with its scattered humping hills. For that matter, to keep it all materialistic, were not some of the atoms shed from de Castries's body during his life and during his burial forty years ago around Franz here at this very moment and in the very air that he was discreetly sniffing in?—atoms being so vastly tiny and infinity-numerous. As were the atoms, too, of Francis Drake (sailing past San Francisco Bay-to-be in the *Golden Hind*) and of Shakespeare and Socrates and Solomon (and of Dashiell Hammett and Clark Ashton Smith). And for that matter, too, had not the atoms that were to become Thibaut de Castries been circulating around the world before the pyramids were built, slowly converging on the spot (in Vermont? in France?) where the old devil would be born? And before that, had not those Thibaut atoms been swiftly vectoring from the violent birthplace of all the universe to the space-time spot where earth would be born and all its weird Pandora woes?

Blocks off, a siren yelped. Nearby, a dark cat darted into a black slit between walls set too close for human passage. It made Franz think of how big buildings had been threatening to crush man ever since the first mega-city had been built. Really Saul's crazy (?) Mrs. Willis wasn't so far off the track, nor Lovecraft (and Smith?)

with his fascinated dread of vast rooms with ceilings that were indoor skies and far walls that were horizons, in buildings vaster still. San Francisco was carbuncled with the latter, and each month new ones grew. Were the signs of the universe written into them? Whose wandering atoms didn't they hold? And were paramentals their personification of their vermin or their natural predators? In any case, it all transpired as logically and ineluctably as the rice-paper journal had passed from Smith, who wrote in purple ink; to de Castries, who added a deadly, secret black; to Ricker, who was a locksmith, not a bibliophile; to Soames, who had a precociously sexy daughter; to Westen, who was susceptible to weird and sexy things.

A dark blue taxi coasting slowly and silently downhill ghosted by Franz, and drew up at the opposite curb.

No wonder Donaldus had wanted Franz to keep the journal and its newfound curse! Byers was an old campaigner against paramentals, with his defense in depth of locks and lights and stars and signs and mazes, and liquor, drugs and sex, and outré sex—Fa Lo Suee had brought Shirley Soames for him as well as for herself; the humorously hostile groping had been to cheer him. Very resourceful, truly. A person had to sleep. Maybe he'd learn, Franz told himself, to use the Byers method himself some day, minus the liquor, but not tonight, no, not until he had to.

The headlights of an unseen car on Noe illuminated the corner ahead at the foot of Beaver. While Franz scanned for shapes that might have been hiding in the dark and now revealed, he thought of Donaldus's inner defense perimeter, meaning his aesthetic approach to life; his theory that art and reality, fiction and nonfiction, were all one, so that one needn't waste energy distinguishing them.

But wasn't even that defense a rationalization, Franz asked himself, an attempt to escape facing the overwhelming question that you're led to: *Are paramentals real?*

Yet how could you answer that question when you were on the run and getting weary and wearier?

And then Franz suddenly saw how he could escape for now, at least buy time in which to think in safety. And it did not involve liquor, drugs, or sex, or diminishing watchfulness in any way. He touched his pocketbook and felt inside it—yes, there was the ticket. He struck a match and glanced at his watch—not yet quite eight, still time enough if he moved swiftly. He turned. The dark blue cab, having discharged its passenger, was coming down Beaver with its hire light on. He stepped into the street and waved it down. He started to get in, then hesitated. A searching glance told him that the dusky, lustrous interior was empty. He got inside and slammed the door, noting approvingly that the windows were closed.

"The Civic Center," he directed. "The Veterans Building. There is a concert there."

"Oh, one of those," the driver said, an older man. "If you don't mind, I won't take Market; it's too torn up. Going around, we'll get there quicker."

"That's fine," Franz said, settling back as the cab turned north on Noe and speeded up. He knew—or had been assuming—that ordinary physical laws didn't apply to paramentals, even if they were real, and so that being in a swiftly moving vehicle didn't make his situation any safer, but it felt that way—it helped.

The familiar drama of a cab ride took hold of him a little—the dark houses and storefronts shooting past, the slowings at the bright corners, the red-green race with the stop lights. But he still kept scanning, regularly swinging his head to look behind, now to the left, now to the right.

"When I was a kid here," the driver said, "they didn't use to tear up Market so much. But now they do it all the time. That BART. And other streets too. All those damn high rises. We'd be better off without them."

"I'm with you there," Franz said.

"You and me both," the driver confirmed. "The driving'd sure be easier. Watch it, you bastard."

The last rather mildly spoken remark was intended for a car that was trying to edge into the right lane on McAllister, though hardly for the ears of its driver. Down a side

street Franz saw a huge orange globe aloft like a Jupiter
that was all one Red Spot—advertisement of a Union 76
gas station. They turned on Van Ness and immediately
drew up at the curb. Franz paid his fare, adding a generous
tip and crossed the wide sidewalk to the Veterans Building
and through its wide glass door into its lofty lobby set with
eight-inch-diameter tubular modernistic sculptures like
giant metal worms at war.

With a few other latecoming concertgoers he hurried to
the elevator at the back, feeling both claustrophobia and
relief as the slow doors closed. On the fourth floor they
joined the press of last-minute folk in the foyer giving up
their tickets and taking their programs before entering the
medium-size high, bone-white concert hall with its check-
ered ceiling and its rows of folding chairs, now mostly
occupied, judging from here.

At first the press of people in the foyer bothered Franz
(anyone might be, or hide, anything) but rather swiftly
began to reassure him by their concert-normality: the
mostly conservative clothes, whether establishment or
hippie; the scatter of elven folk in arty garb suitable for
rarefied artistic experiences; the elderly groups, the ladies
in sober evening dresses with a touch of silver, the gentle-
men rather fussily clad at collars and cuffs. One young
couple held Franz's attention for more than a moment.
They were both small and delicately made, both of them
looking scrupulously clean. They were dressed in very
well tailored brand-new hippie garb: he in leathern jacket
and corduroy trews, she in a beautifully faded blue denim
suit with large pale splotches. They looked like children,
but his neatly trimmed beard and the demure outdenting of
her tender bosom proclaimed them adult. They held hands
rather like dolls, as if they were used to handling each
other very carefully. One thought of prince and prin-
cess on a masquerade planned and supervised by gray-
beards.

A very aware and coldly calculating section of Franz's
mind told him that he was not one bit safer here than out in
the dark. Nevertheless his fears were being lulled as they

had been when he'd first arrived at Beaver Street and later, a little, in the cab.

And then, just before entering the concert hall, he glimpsed at the far end of the foyer the backs of a rather small man, gray-haired, in evening dress and a tall slender woman in a beige turban and pale brown, flowing gown. They seemed to be talking animatedly together and as they swiftly turned toward him, he felt an icy chill, for the woman appeared to be wearing a black veil. Then he saw that she was black, while the man's face was somewhat porcine.

As he plunged ahead nervously into the concert hall, he heard his name called, started, then hurried down an aisle to where Gunnar and Saul were holding a seat between them in the third row.

"It's about time," Saul said darkly as Franz edged past.

As he sat down, Gun said from the seat just beyond, grinning somewhat thinly and momentarily laying his hand on Franz's forearm, "We were beginning to get afraid you weren't coming. You know how much Cal depends on you, don't you?" Then a puzzled question came into his face when the glass in Franz's pocket clashed as he pulled his jacket round.

"I broke my binoculars on Corona Heights," Franz said shortly. "I'll tell you about it later." Then a tought came to him. "Do you know much about optics, Gun? Practical optics—instruments and such, prisms and lenses?"

"A little," Gun replied, with an inquiring frown. "And I've a friend who's very much into it. But why—?"

Franz said slowly, "Would it be possible to gimmick a terrestrial telescope, or a pair of binoculars, so a person would see something in the distance that wasn't there?"

"Well . . ." Gunnar began, his expression wondering, his hands making a small gesture of uncertainty. Then he smiled. "Of course, if you tried to look through broken binoculars, I suppose you'd see something like a kaleidoscope."

"Taffy get rough?" Saul asked from the other side.

"Never mind now," Franz told Gunnar and with a quick, temporizing grimace at Saul (and a quick glance behind him and to either side—crowded concertgoers and their coats made such an effective stalking ground), he looked toward the stage, where the half dozen or so instrumentalists were already seated—in a shallow, concave curve just beyond the conductor's podium, one of the strings still tuning thoughtfully. The long and narrow shape of the harpsichord, its slim bench empty, made the left end of the curve, somewhat downstage to favor its small tones.

Franz looked at his program. The Brandenburg Fifth was the finale. There were two intermissions. The concert opened with:

Concerto in C Major
   for Harpsichord and
   Chamber Orchestra
   by Giovanni Paisiello
     1. Allegro
     2. Larghetto
     3. Allegro (Rondo)

Saul nudged him. He looked up. Cal had come on stage unobtrusively. She wore a white evening frock that left her shoulders bare and sparkled just a little at the edges. She said something to a woodwind, and in turning, looked the audience over without making a point of it. He thought she saw him, but he couldn't be sure. She seated herself. The house lights went down. To a spreading ripple of applause the conductor entered, took his place, looked around from under his eyebrows at his instrumentalists, tapped the lectern with his wand, and raised it sharply.

Beside Franz, Saul murmured prayerfully, "Now in the name of Bach and Sigmund Freud, give 'em hell, Calpurnia."

"And of Pythagoras," Gun faintly chimed.

The sweet and rocking music of the strings and of the

softly calling, lulling woodwinds enfolded Franz. For the first time since Corona Heights he felt wholly safe, among his friends and in the arms of ordered sound, as if the music were an intimate crystal heaven around and over them, a perfect barrier to paranatural forces.

But then the harpsichord came in challengingly, banishing cradled sleep, its sparkling and shivery ribbons of high sound propounding questions and gaily yet inflexibly commanding that they be answered. The harpsichord told Franz that the concert hall was every bit as much an escape as anything proposed on Beaver Street.

Before he knew what he was doing, though not until he knew well what he was feeling, Franz had got stoopingly to his feet and was edging out in front of Saul, intensely conscious yet regardless of the waves of shock, protest, and condemnation silently focused upon him from the audience—or so he fancied.

He only paused to bend his lips close to Saul's ear and say softly but very distinctly, "Tell Cal—but only after she's played the Brandenburg—that her music made me go to find the answer to the 607 Rhodes question," and then he was edging on quite rapidly, the back of his left hand very lightly brushing backs to steady his course, his right hand an apologetic shield between himself and the sitters he passed in front of.

As he reached the end of the row, he looked back once and saw Saul's frowning and intensely speculative face, framed by his long brown hair, fixed upon him. Then he was hurrying up the aisle between the hostile rows, lashed on—as if by a whip strung with thousands of tiny diamonds—by the music of the harpsichord, which never faltered. He kept his gaze fixed steadily ahead.

He wondered why he'd said "the 607 Rhodes question" instead of "the question of whether paramentals are real," but then he realized it was because it was a question Cal had herself asked more than once and so might catch its drift. It was important that she understand that he was working.

He was tempted to take a last look back, but didn't.

24

IN THE STREET outside the Veterans Building, Franz resumed his sidewise and backward peerings, now somewhat randomized, yet he was conscious not so much of fear as of wariness, as if he were a savage on a mission in a concrete jungle, traveling along the bottoms of perilously walled, rectilineal gorges. Having taken a deliberate plunge into danger, he felt almost cocky.

He headed over two blocks and then up Larkin, walking rapidly yet not noisily. The passersby were few. The gibbous moon was almost overhead. Up Turk a siren yelped some blocks away. He kept up his swiveling watch for the paramental of his binoculars and/or for Thibaut's ghost—perhaps a material ghost formed of Thibaut's floating ashy remains, or a portion of them. Such things might not be real, there still might be a natural explanation (or he might be crazy), but until he was sure of one or the other, it was only good sense to stay on guard.

Down Ellis the slot which held his favorite tree was black, but streetside its fingered branch-ends were green in the white street lights.

A half-dozen blocks west on O'Farrell he glimpsed the modernistic bulk of St. Mary's Cathedral, pale gray in the moonlight, and wondered uneasily about another Lady.

He turned down Geary past dark shop fronts, two lighted bars, and the wide yawning mouth of the De Soto garage, home of the blue taxicabs, and came to the dingy white awning that marked 811.

Inside the lobby there were a couple of rough-looking male types sitting on the ledge of small hexagonal marble

tiles below the two rows of brass mailboxes. Probably
drunk. They followed him with their dull eyes as he took
the elevator.

He got off at six and closed the two elevator doors
quietly (the folding latticed and the solid one) and walked
softly past the black window and the black broom closet
door with its gaping round hole where the knob would
have been, and stopped in front of his own door.

After listening a short while and hearing nothing, he
unlocked it with two twists of his key and stepped inside,
feeling a burst of excitement and fear. This time he did not
switch on the bright ceiling light, but only stood listening
and intent, waiting for his eyes to accommodate.

The room was full of darkness. Outside the open window the night was pale (dark gray, rather) with the moon
and with the indirect glow of the city's lights. Everything
was very quiet except for the faint, distant rumbles and
growls of traffic and the rushing of his blood. Suddenly
there came through the pipes a solid, low roaring as
someone turned on water a floor or two away. It stopped
as suddenly and the inside silence returned.

Adventurously, Franz shut the door and felt his way
along the wall and around the tall clothes cabinet, carefully avoiding the work-laden coffee table, to the head of his
bed, where he turned on the light. He ran his gaze along
his Scholar's Mistress, lying slim, dark, and inscrutably
silent against the wall, and on to the open casement
window.

Two yards inside it, the large oblong of fluorescent red
cardboard lay on the floor. He walked over and picked it
up. It was jaggedly bent down the middle and a little
ragged at the corners. He shook his head, set it against the
wall, and went back to the window. Two torn corners of
cardboard were still tacked to the window sides. The
drapes hung tidily. There were crumbles and tiny shreds
of pale brownish paper on his narrow desk and the floor at
his feet. He couldn't remember whether or not he'd
cleaned up those from yesterday. He noted that the neat

little stack of ungutted old pulps was gone. Had he put those away somewhere? He couldn't remember that either.

Conceivably a very strong gust of wind could have torn out the red cardboard, but wouldn't it also have disordered the drapes and blown the paper crumbs off his desk? He looked out to the red lights of the TV tower; thirteen of them small and steady, six brighter and flashing. Below them, a mile closer, the dark hump of Corona Heights was outlined by the city's yellowish window and street lights and a few bright whites and greens in snaky curves. Again he shook his head.

He rapidly searched his place, this time not feeling foolish. In the closet and clothes cabinet he swung the hanging garments aside and glanced behind them. He noticed a pale gray raincoat of Cal's from weeks back. He looked behind the shower curtain and under the bed.

On the table between the closet and bathroom doors lay his unopened mail. Topmost was a cancer drive letter from an organization he'd contributed to after Daisy had died. He frowned and momentarily narrowed his lips, his face compressed with pain. Beside the little pile were a small slate, some pieces of white chalk, and his prisms, with which he occasionally played with sunlight, splitting it into spectrums, and into spectrums of spectrums. He called to his Scholar's Mistress, -'We'll have you in gay clothes again, just like a rainbow, my dear, after all this is over.''

He got a city map and a ruler and went to his couch, where he fished his broken binoculars out of his pocket and set them carefully on an unpiled edge of the coffee table. It gave him a feeling of safety to think that now the snout-faced paramental couldn't get to him without crossing broken glass, like that which they used to cement atop walls to keep out intruders—until he realized just how illogical that was.

He took out Smith's journal too and settled himself beside his Scholar's Mistress, spreading out the map.

Then he opened the journal to de Castries's curse, marveling again that it had so long eluded him, and reread the crucial portion:

> The fulcrum (0) and the Cipher (A) shall be here, at his *beloved* 607 Rhodes. I'll be at rest in my appointed spot (1) under the Bishop's Seat, the heaviest ashes that he ever felt. Then when the weights are on at Sutro Mount (4) and Monkey Clay (5) [(4) + (1) = (5)] *BE his Life Squeezed Away*.

Now to work out, he told himself, this problem in black geometry, or would it be black physics? What had Byers said Klaas had said de Castries had called it? Oh, yes, Neo-Pythagorean metageometry.

Monkey Clay was the most incongruous item in the curse, all right. Start here. Donaldus had maundered about simian and human clay, but that led nowhere. It ought to be a *place*, like Mount Sutro—or Corona Heights (under the Bishop's Seat). Clay was a street in San Francisco. But Monkey?

Franz's mind took a leap from Monkey Clay to Monkey Wards. Why? He'd known a man who'd worked at Sears Roebuck's great rival and who said he and some of his lowly coworkers called their company that.

Another leap, from Monkey Wards to the Monkey Block. Of course! The Monkey Block was the proudly derisive name of a huge old San Francisco apartment building, long torn down, where bohemians and artists had lived cheaply in the Roaring Twenties and the Depression years. Monkey—short for the street it was on— Montgomery! Another San Francisco street, and one crosswise to Clay! (There was something more than that, but his mind hung fire and he couldn't wait.)

He excitedly laid the ruler on the flattened map between Mount Sutro and the intersection of Clay and Montgomery Streets in the north end of the financial district. He saw that the straight line so indicated went through the middle of Corona Heights! (And also rather close by the intersection of Geary and Hyde, he noted with a little grimace.)

He took a pencil from the coffee table and marked a small "five" at the Montgomery-Clay intersection, a "four" by Mount Sutro, and a "one" in the middle of Corona Heights. He noted that the straight line became like a balance or scales then (two lever arms) with the balancing point or fulcrum somewhere between Corona Heights and Montgomery-Clay. It even balanced mathematically: four plus one equals five—just as was noted in the curse before the final injunction. That miserable fulcrum (0), wherever it was, would surely be pressed to death by those two great lever arms ("Give me a place to stand and I will stomp the world to death"— Archimedes) just as that poor little lower-case "his" was crushed between that dreadful *"BE"* and the three big capitalized words.

Yes, that unfortunate (0) would surely be suffocated, compressed to a literal nothing, especially when "the weights" were "on." Now what—?

Suddenly it occurred to Franz that whatever had been the case in the past, the weights were certainly on *now*, with the TV tower standing three-legged on Mount Sutro and with Montgomery-Clay the location of the Trans-america Pyramid, San Francisco's tallest building! (The "something else" was that the Monkey Block had been torn down to clear a site first for a parking lot, then for the Transamerica Pyramid. Closer and closer!)

That was why the curse hadn't got Smith. He'd died before either structure had been built. The trap hadn't become set until *later*.

The Transamerica Pyramid and the 1,000-foot TV tower—those were crushers, all right.

But it was ridiculous to think that de Castries could have predicted the building of those structures. And in any case coincidence—lucky hits—was an adequate explana-tion. Pick any intersection in downtown San Francisco and there was at least a 50 percent chance of there being a high rise there, or nearby.

But why was he holding his breath then; why was there

a faint roaring in his ears; why were his fingers cold and tingling?

Why had de Castries told Klaas and Ricker that prescience, or foreknowledge, was possible at certain spots in mega-cities? Why had he named his book (it lay beside Franz now, a dirty gray) *Megapolisomancy*?

Whatever the truth behind, the weights certainly were on now, no question.

Which made it all the more important to find out the real location of that baffling 607 Rhodes where the old devil had lived (dragged out the tail end of his life) and Smith had asked his questions . . . and where, according to the curse, the ledger containing the Grand Cipher was hidden . . . and where the curse would be fulfilled. Really, it was quite like a detective story. By Dashiell Hammett? "X marks the spot" where the victim was (will be?) discovered, crushed to death? They'd put up a brass plaque at Bush and Stockton near where Brigid O'Shaunnesy had shot Miles Archer in Hammett's *The Maltese Falcon*, but there were no memorials for Thibaut de Castries, a real person. Where was the elusive X, or mystic (0)? Where *was* 607 Rhodes? Really, he should have asked Byers when he'd the chance. Call him up now? No, he'd severed his connection there. Beaver Street was an area he didn't want to venture back to, even by phone. At least for now. But he left off poring over the map as futile.

His gaze fell on the 1927 San Francisco City Directory he'd ripped off that morning that formed the midsection of his Scholar's Mistress. Might as well finish that bit of research right now—find the name of this building, if it ever had one, if it had, indeed, become a listed hotel. He heaved the thick volume onto his lap and turned the dingily yellowed pages to the "Hotels" section. At another time he'd have been amused by the old advertisements for patent medicines and barber parlors.

He thought of all the searching around he'd done this morning at the Civic Center. It all seemed very far off now and quite naive.

Let's see, the best way would be to search through the addresses, not for Geary Street—there'd be a lot of hotels on Geary—but for 811. There'd probably be only one of those if any. He began running a fingernail down the first column rather slowly, but steadily.

He was on the next to last column before he came to an 811. Yes, it was Geary too, all right. The name was . . . the Rhodes Hotel.

25

FRANZ FOUND HIMSELF standing in the hall facing his closed door. His body was trembling very slightly all over—a general fine tremor.

Then he realized why he had come out here. It was to check the number on the door, the small dark oblong on which was incised in pale gray, "607." He wanted to see it actually and to see his room from the outside (and incidentally dissociate himself from the curse, get off the target).

He got the feeling that if he knocked just now (as Clark Smith must have knocked so many times on this same door) Thibaut de Castries would open it, his sunk-cheeked face a webwork of fine gray wrinkles as if it has been powdered with fine ashes.

If he went back in without knocking, it would be as he'd left it. But if he knocked, then the old spider would wake . . .

He felt vertigo, as if the building were beginning to lean over with him inside it, to rotate ever so slowly, at least at first. The feeling was like earthquake panic.

He had to orient himself at once, he told himself, to keep himself from falling over with 811. He went down the dark hall (the bulb inside the globe over the elevator door was still out) past the black broom closet, the black-painted window of the airshaft, the elevator itself, and softly up the stairs two flights, gripping the banister to keep his balance, and under the peaked skylight of the stairwell into the sinister black room that housed under a larger skylight the elevator's motor and relays, the Green

Dwarf and the Spider, and so out onto the tarred and graveled roof.

The stars were in the sky where they should be, though naturally dimmed somewhat by the glare of the gibbous moon, which was in the top of the sky a little to the south. Orion and Aldebaran climbed the east. Polaris was at his unchanging spot. All round about stretched the angular horizon, crenelated with high rises and skyscrapers marked rather sparsely with red warning and yellow window lights, as if somewhat aware of the need to conserve energy. A moderate wind was from the west.

His dizziness gone at least, Franz moved toward the back of the roof, past the mouths of the air shafts that were like walled square wells, and watchful for the low vent pipes covered with heavy wire netting that were so easy to trip over, until he stood at the roof's west edge above his room and Cal's. One of his hands rested on the low wall. Off a short way behind him was the airshaft that dropped straight down by the black window he'd passed in the hall and the corresponding ones above and below it on the other floors. Opening on the same shaft, he recalled, were the bathroom windows of another set of apartments and also a vertical row of quite small windows that could only let into the disused broom closets, originally to give them some light, he supposed. He looked west at the flashing reds of the Tower and at the irregularly rounded darkness of the Heights. The wind freshened a little.

He thought at last, this is the Rhodes Hotel. I live at 607 Rhodes, the place I've hunted for everywhere else. There's really no mystery at all about it. Behind me is the Transamerica Pyramid (5). (He looked over his shoulder at it where its single red light flashed bright and its lighted windows were as narrow as the holes in a business-machine card.) In front of me (he turned back) are the TV tower (4) and the crowned and hunchbacked eminence (1) where the old spider king's ashes lie buried, as they say. And I am at the fulcrum (0) of the curse.

As he fatalistically told himself that, the stars seemed to grow dimmer still, a sickly pallor, and he felt a sickness and a heaviness within himself and all around, as if the freshening wind had blown something malignant out of the west to this dark roof, as if some universal disease or cosmic pollution were spiraling from Corona Heights to the whole cityscape and so up to the stars, infecting even Orion and the Shield—as if with the stars' help he'd been getting things in place and now something was refusing to stay in its appointed spot, refusing to stay buried and forgotten, like Daisy's cancer, and interfering with the rule of number and order in the universe.

He heard a sudden scuffing and scuttling sound behind him and he spun around. Nothing there, nothing that he could see, and yet . . .

He moved to the nearest airshaft and looked down. Moonlight penetrated it as far as his floor, where the little window to the broom closet was open. Below that, it was very dimly lit from two of the bathroom windows— indirect light seeping from the living rooms of those apartments. He heard a sound as of an animal snuffing, or was that his own heavy breathing reflected by the echoing sheet-iron? And he fancied he saw (but it was very dim) something with rather too many limbs moving about, rapidly down and up.

He jerked his head back and then up, as if looking to the stars for help, but they seemed as lonely and uncaring as the very distant windows a lone man sees who is about to be murdered on a moor or sink into the Great Grimpen Marsh at dead of night. Panic seized him and he rushed back the way he'd come. As he passed through the black room of the elevator, the big copper switches snapped loudly and the relay arms clashed grindingly, hurrying his flight as if there were a monster Spider snapping at his heels at a Green Dwarf's groaning commands.

He got some control of himself going down the stairs, but on his own floor as he passed the black-painted window (near the dark ceiling globe) he got the feeling there was something supremely agile crouched against the other side of it, clinging in the airshaft, something midway between a black panther and a spider monkey, but perhaps as many-limbed as a spider and perhaps with the creviced, ashen face of Thibaut de Castries, about to burst in through the wire-toughened glass. As he passed the black door of the broom closet, he remembered the small window opening from it into the shaft, that would not be too small for such a creature. And now the broom closet itself was right up against the wall that ran along the inside of his couch. How many of us in a big city, he asked himself, know anything about what lies in or just on the other side of the outer walls of our apartments—often the very wall against which we sleep?—as hidden and unreachable as our internal organs. We can't even trust the walls that guard us.

In the hall, the broom closet door seemed suddenly to bulge. For a frantic moment he thought he'd left his keys in his room, then he found them in his pocket and located the right one on the ring and got the door open and himself inside and the door double-locked behind him against whatever might have followed him from the roof.

But could he trust his room with its open window? No matter how unreachable the latter was in theory. He searched the place again, this time finding himself impelled to view each volume of space. Even pulling the file drawers out and peering behind the folders did not make him feel embarrassed. He searched his clothes cabinet last and so thoroughly that he discovered on its floor against the wall behind some boots an unopened bottle of kirschwasser he must have squirreled away there over a year ago when he was still drinking.

He glanced toward the window with its crumbles of ancient paper and found himself picturing de Castries when he'd lived here. The old spider had doubtless sat before the window for long hours, viewing his grave-to-be on Corona Heights with forested Mount Sutro beyond. And had he previsioned the tower that would rise there? The old spiritualists and occultists believed that the astral remains, the odic dust, of a person lingered on in rooms where he'd lived.

What else had the old spider dreamed about there?

rocking his body in the chair a little. His days of glory in pre-Earthquake Frisco? The men and women he had teased to suicide, or tucked under various fulcrums to be crushed? His father (Afric adventurer or hayseed printer), his black panther (if he'd ever had one, let alone several) his young Polish mistress (or slim girl-Anima), his Veiled Lady?

If only there were someone to talk to and free him from these morbid thoughts! If only Cal and the others would get back from the concert. But his wristwatch indicated that it was only a few minutes past nine. Hard to believe his room searches and roof visit had taken so little time, but the second hand of his wristwatch was sweeping around steadily in almost imperceptibly tiny jerks.

The thought of the lonely hours ahead made him feel desperate and the bottle in his hand with its white promise of oblivion tempted him, but the dread of what might happen when he had made himself unarousable was still greater.

He set the cherry brandy down beside yesterday's mail, also still unopened, and his prisms and slate. He'd thought the last was blank, but now he fancied he saw faint marks on it. He took it and the chalk and prisms lying on it over to the lamp at the head of his couch. He'd thought of switching on the 200-watt ceiling light, but somehow he didn't like the idea of having his window stand out that glaringly bright, perhaps for a watcher on Corona Heights.

There *were* spidery chalk marks on the slate—a half dozen faint triangles that narrowed toward the downward corner, as if someone or some force had been lightly outlining (the chalk perhaps moving like the planchette of a ouija board) the snouted face of his paramental. And now the chalk and one of the prisms *were* jumping about like planchettes, his hands holding the slate were shaking so.

His mind was almost paralyzed—almost blanked—by sudden fear, but a free corner of it was thinking how a white five-pointed star with one point directed *upward* (or

outward) is supposed in witchcraft to protect a room from
the entry of evil spirits as if the invading entity would be
spiked on the star's upward (or outward) point, and so he
was hardly surprised when he found that he'd put down
the slate on the end of his piled coffee table and was
chalking such stars on the sills of his windows, the open
one and the locked one in the bathroom, and above his
door. He felt distantly ridiculous, but didn't even consider
not completing the stars. In fact, his imagination ran on to
the possibility of even more secret passageways and hiding places in the building than the airshafts and broom
closets (there would have been a dumbwaiter and a laundry chute in the Rhodes Hotel and who knows what
auxiliary doors) and he became bothered that he couldn't
inspect the back walls of the closet and clothes cabinet
more clearly, and in the end he closed the doors of both
and chalked a star above them—and a small star above the
transom.

He was considering chalking one more star on the wall
by his couch where it abutted the broom closet in the hall,
when there sounded at his door a sharp *knock-knock*. He
put on the chain before he opened it the two inches which
that allowed.

26

HALF OF A toothy mouth and large brown eye were grinning up at him across the chain and a voice saying, "E-chess?"

Franz quickly unhooked the chain and opened the door eagerly. He was vastly relieved to have a familiar person with him, sharply disappointed that it was someone with whom he could hardly communicate at all—certainly not the stuff crowding his mind—yet consoled by the thought that at least they shared the language of chess. Chess would at least pass some time, he hoped.

Fernando came in beaming, though frowning questioningly a moment at the chain, and then again at Franz when he quickly reclosed and double locked the door.

In answer, Franz offered him a drink. Fernando's black eyebrows went up at sight of the square bottle, and he smiled wider and nodded, but when Franz had opened the bottle and poured him a small wineglass, he hesitated, asking with his mobile features and expressive hands why Franz wasn't drinking.

As the simplest solution, Franz poured himself a bit in another wineglass, hiding with his fingers how little, and tilted the glass until the aromatic liquid wet his closed lips. He offered Fernando a second drink, but the latter pointed towards the chessmen, then at his head, which he shook smilingly.

Franz set the chessboard somewhat precariously on top of the piled folders on the coffee table, and sat down on the bed. Fernando looked somewhat dubiously at the arrangement, then shrugged and smiled, drew up a chair and sat down opposite. He got the white pawn and when they'd set up the men he opened confidently.

Franz made his moves quickly, too. He found himself almost automatically resuming the "on guard" routine he'd employed at Beaver Street while listening to Byers. His watchful gaze would move from the end of the wall behind him to his clothes cabinet to the door, then past a small bookcase to the closet door, across the table crowded with the unopened mail and all, past the bathroom door to the larger bookcase and desk, pause at the window, then travel along his filing cabinets to the steam radiator and to the other end of the wall behind him, then start back again. He got the ghost of a bitter taste as he wet his lips— the kirschwasser.

Fernando won in twenty moves or so. He looked thoughtfully at Franz for a couple of moments, as if about to make some point about his indifferent play, but instead smiled and began to set up the men with colors reversed.

With deliberate recklessness Franz opened with the king's gambit. Fernando countered in the center with his queen's pawn. Despite the dangerous and chancy position, Franz found he couldn't concentrate on the game. He kept searching his mind for other precautions to take besides his visual guard. He strained his ears for sounds at the door and beyond the other partitions. He wished desperately that Fernando had more English, or weren't so deaf. The combination was simply too much.

And the time passed so slowly. The large hand of his wristwatch was frozen. It was like one of those moments at a drunken party—when you're on the verge of blackout—that seem to last forever. At this rate it would be ages before the concert was over.

And then it occurred to him that he had no guarantee that Cal and the others would return at once. People generally went to bars or restaurants after performances, to celebrate or talk.

He was faintly aware of Fernando studying him between the moves.

Of course he could go back to the concert himself when

Fernando left. But that wouldn't settle anything. He'd left
the concert determined to solve the problem of de Castries's curse and all the strangeness that went with it. And
at least he'd made progress. He'd already answered the
literal 607 Rhodes question, but of course he'd meant a lot
more than that when he'd spoken to Saul.

But how could he find the answer to the whole thing
anyway? Serious psychic or occult research was a matter
of elaborate preparation and study, using delicate, carefully checked-out instruments, or at any rate sensitive,
trained people salted by previous experience: mediums,
sensitives, telepaths, clairvoyants and such—who'd
proved themselves with Rhine cards and what not. What
could he hope to do just by himself in one evening? What
had he been thinking of when he'd walked out on Cal's
concert and left her that message?

Yet somehow he had the feeling that all the physical
research experts and their massed experience wouldn't
really be a bit of help to him now. Any more than the
science experts would be with their incredibly refined
electronic and radionic detectors and photography and
whatnot. That amid all the fields of occult and fringe-
occult that were flourishing today—witchcraft, astrology,
biofeedback, dowsing, psychokinesis, auras, acupunc-
ture, exploratory LSD trips, loops in the time stream,
astrology (much of them surely fake, some of them maybe
real)—this that was happening to him was altogether
different.

He pictured himself going back to the concert, and he
didn't like the picture. Very faintly, he seemed to hear the
swift, glittery music of a harpsichord, still luring and
lashing him on imperiously.

Fernando cleared his throat. Franz realized he'd overlooked a mate in three moves and had lost the second
game in as few moves as the first. He automatically
started to set up the pieces for a third.

Fernando's hand, palm down in an emphatic no, prevented him. Franz looked up.

Fernando was looking intently at him. The Peruvian

frowned and shook a finger at Franz, indicated he was concerned about him. Then he pointed at the chessboard, then at his own head, touching his temple. Then he shook his head decisively, frowning and pointing toward Franz again.

Franz got the message: "Your mind is not on the game." He nodded.

Fernando stood up, pushing his chair out of the way, and pantomimed a man afraid of something that was after him. Crouching a little, he kept looking around, much as Franz had been doing, but more obviously. He kept turning and looking suddenly behind him, now in one direction, now the other, his face big-eyed and fearful.

Franz nodded that he got it.

Fernando moved around the room, darting quick glances at the hall door and the window. While looking in another direction he rapped loudly on the radiator with his clenched fist, then instantly gave a great start and backed off from it.

A man very afraid of something, startled by sudden noises, that must mean. Franz nodded again.

Fernando did the same thing with the bathroom door and with the nearby wall. After rapping on the latter he stared at Franz and said, "*Hay hechiceria. Hechiceria ocultado en murallas.*"

What had Cal said that meant? "Witchcraft, witchcraft hidden in walls." Franz recalled his own wonderings about secret doors and chutes and passageways. But did Fernando mean it literally or figuratively? Franz nodded, but pursed his lips and otherwise tried to put on a questioning look.

Fernando appeared to notice the chalked stars for the first time. White on pale woodwork, they weren't easy to see. His eyebrows went up and he smiled understandingly at Franz and nodded approvingly. He indicated the stars and then held his hands out, palms flat and away from him, at the window and doors, as if keeping something out, holding it at bay—meanwhile continuing to nod approvingly.

"*Bueno*," he said.

Franz nodded, at the same time marveling at the fear that had led him to snatch at such an irrational protective device, one that the superstition-sodden (?) Fernando understood instantly—stars against witches. (And there had been five-pointed stars among the graffiti on Corona Heights, intended to keep dead bones at rest and ashes quiet. Byers had sprayed them there.)

He stood up and went to the table and offered Fernando another drink, uncapping the bottle, but Fernando refused it with a short crosswise wave of his hand, palm down, and crossed to where Franz had been and rapped on the wall behind the couch and turning toward Franz repeated, "*Hechiceria ocultado en muralla!*"

Franz looked at him questioningly. But the Peruvian only bowed his head and put three fingers to his forehead, symbolizing thought (and possibly the Peruvian was actually thinking, too).

Then Fernando looked up with an air of revelation, took the chalk from the slate beside the chessboard, and drew on the wall a five-pointed star, larger and more conspicuous and better than any of Franz's.

"*Bueno*," Fernando said again, nodding. Then he pointed down behind the bed toward the baseboard it hid, repeated, "*Hay hechiceria en muralla*," and went quickly to the hall door and pantomimed himself going away and coming back, and then looked at Franz solicitously, lifting his eyebrows, as if to ask, "You'll be all right in the meantime?"

Rather bemused by the pantomime and feeling suddenly quite weary, Franz nodded with a smile and (thinking of the star Fernando had drawn and the feeling of fellowship it had given him) said, "*Gracias*."

Fernando nodded with a smile, unbolted the door, and went out, shutting the door behind him. A little later Franz heard the elevator stop at this floor, its doors open and close, and go droning down, as if headed for the basement of the universe.

27

FRANZ FELT A little as though he imagined a punchdrunk boxer would. His ears and eyes were still on guard, tracking the faintest sounds and slightest sights, but tiredly, almost protestingly, fighting the urge to slump. Despite all the day's shocks and surprises, his evening mind (slave of his body's chemistry) was taking over. Presumably Fernando had gone somewhere—but why? to fetch what?—and eventually would come back as he'd pantomimed—but how soon? and again why? Truly, Franz didn't much care. He began rather automatically to tidy around him.

Soon he sat down with a weary sigh on the side of his bed and stared at the incredibly piled and crowded coffee table, wondering where to start. At the bottom was his neatly layered current writing work, which he'd hardly looked at or thought of since day before yesterday. *Weird Underground*—it was ironic. Atop that were the phone on its long cord, his broken binoculars, his big, tar-blackened, overflowing ashtray (but he hadn't smoked since he'd got in tonight and wasn't moved to now), the chessboard with its men half set up, beside it the flat slate with its chalk, his prisms, and some captured chess pieces, and finally the tiny wineglasses and the square bottle of kirschwasser, still uncapped, where he'd set it down after offering it a last time to Fernando.

Gradually the whole jumbled arrangement began to seem drolly amusing to Franz, quite beyond dealing with. Although his eyes and ears were still tracking automatically (and kept on doing so) he almost giggled weakly. His evening mind invariably had its silly side, a tendency toward puns and oddly mixed clichés, and faintly psychotic epigrams—foolishness born of fatigue. He recalled how neatly the psychologist F.C. MacKnight had described the transition from waking to sleeping: the mind's short logical daytime steps becoming longer by degrees, each mental jump a little more farfetched and wild, until (with never a break) they were utterly unpredictable giant strides and one was dreaming.

He picked up the city map from where he'd left it spread on his bed and without folding it he laid it as if it were a coverlet atop the clutter on the coffee table.

"Go to sleep, little junk pile," he said with humorous tenderness.

And he laid the ruler he'd been using on top of that, like a magician relinquishing his wand.

Then (his ears and eyes still doing their guard rounds) he half-turned to the wall where Fernando had chalked the star and began to put his books to bed too, as he had the mess on the coffee table, began to tuck in his Scholar's Mistress for the night, as it were—a homely operation on familiar things that was the perfect antidote even to wildest fears.

Upon the yellowed, brown-edged pages of *Megapolisomancy*—the section about "electro-mephitic city-stuff"—he gently laid Smith's journal, open at the curse.

"You're very pale, my dear," he observed (the rice paper), "and yet the left-hand side of your face has all those very odd black beauty marks, a whole page of them. Dream of a lovely Satanist party in full evening dress, all white and black like *Marienbad*, in an angelfood ballroom with creamy slim borzois stepping about like courteous giant spiders."

He touched a shoulder that was chiefly Lovecraft's *Outsider*, its large forty-year-old Winnebago Eggshell pages open at "The Thing on the Doorstep." He murmured to his mistress, "Don't deliquesce now, dear, like poor Asenath Waite. Remember, you've got no dental work (that I know of) by which you could be positively identified." He glanced at the other shoulder: coverless, crumble-edged *Wonder Stories* and *Weird Tales*, with Smith's "The Disinterment of Venus" spread at the top. "That's a far better way to go," he commented. "All rosy marble under the worms and mold."

The chest was Ms. Lettland's monumental book, rather appropriately open at that mysterious, provocative, and question-raising chapter, "The Mammary Mystique: Cold as . . ." He thought of the feminist author's strange disappearance in Seattle. Now no one ever could know her further answers.

His fingers trailed across the rather slender, black, gray-mottled waist made of James's ghost stories—the book had once been thoroughly rained on and then been laboriously dried out, page by forever wrinkled, discolored page—and he straightened a little the stolen city directory (representing hips), still open at the hotels section, saying quietly, "There, that'll be more comfortable for you. You know, dear friend, you're doubly 607 Rhodes now," and wondered rather dully what he meant by that.

He heard the elevator stop outside and its doors open, but didn't hear it going off again. He waited tautly, but there was no knock at his door, no footsteps in the hall that he could hear. There came from somewhere through the wall the faint jar of a stubborn door being quietly opened or closed, then nothing more of that.

He touched *The Spider Glyph in Time* where it was lying just below the directory. Earlier in the day his Scholar's Mistress had been lying on her face, but now on her back. He mused a moment (What had Lettland said?) as to why the exterior female genitalia were thought of as a spider. The tendriled blot of hair? The mouth that opened vertically like a spider's jaws instead of horizontally like the human face's lips or the labia of the Chinagirls of sailors' legendry? Old fever-racked Santos-Lobos suggested it involved the time to spin a web, the spider's clock. And what a charming cranny for a cobweb.

His feather-touching fingers moved on to *Knochen-mädchen in Pelze (Mit Peitsche)*—more of the dark hairiness, now changing to soft fur (furs rather) wrapping the skeleton girls—and *Ames et Fantômes de Douleur*, the other thigh; de Sade (or his posthumous counterfeiter), tiring of the flesh, had really wanted to make the mind scream and the angels sob; shouldn't *The Ghosts of Pain* be *The Agonies of Ghosts*?

That book, taken along with Masoch's *Skeleton Girls in Furs (With Whips)*, made him think of what a wealth of death was here under his questing hands. Lovecraft dying quite swiftly in 1937, writing determinedly until the end, taking notes on his last sensations. (Did he see paramentals then?) Smith going more slowly some quarter-century later, his brain nibbled by little strokes. Santos-Lobos burned by his fevers to a thinking cinder. And was vanished Lettland dead? Montague there (his *White Tape* made a knee, only its paper was getting yellow) drowning by emphysema while he still wrote footnotes upon our self-suffocating culture.

Death and the fear of death! Franz recalled how deeply Lovecraft's "The Color Out of Space" had depressed him when he'd read it in his teens—the New England farmer had his family rotting away alive, poisoned by radioactives from the ends of the universe. Yet at the same time it had been so fascinating. What was the whole literature of supernatural horror but an essay to make death itself exciting?—wonder and strangeness to life's very end. But even as he thought that, he realized how tired he was. Tired, depressed, and morbid—the unpleasant aspects of his evening mind, the dark side of its coin.

And speaking of darkness, where did Our Lady of Same fit in? (*Suspiria de Profundis* made the other knee and *De Profundis* a calf. "How do you feel about Lord Alfred Douglas, my dear? Does he turn you on? I think Oscar was much too good for him.") Was the TV tower out there in the night her statue?—it was tall enough and turreted. Was night her 'treble veil of crape?' and the nineteen reds, winking or steady, 'the fierce light of a blazing misery?' Well, he was miserable enough himself for two. Make her laugh at that. Come, sweet night, and pall me.

He finished tucking in his Scholar's Mistress—Prof. Nostig's *The Subliminal Occult* ("You disposed of Kirlian photography, doctor, but could you do as well with the paranatural?"), the copies of *Gnostica* (any relation to Prof. Nostig?), *The Mauritzius Case* (did Etzel Andergast see paramentals in Berlin? and Waramme smokier ones in Chicago?), *Hecate, or the Future of Witchcraft* by Yeats ("Why did you have that book destroyed, William Butler?"), and *Journey to the End of the Night* ("And to your toes, my dear.")—and wearily stretched himself out beside her, *still* stubbornly watchful for the tiniest suspicious sounds and sights. It occurred to him how he had come home to her at night as to a real wife or woman, to be relaxed and comforted after all the tensions, trials, and dangers (Remember they were still there!) of the day.

It occurred to him that he could probably still catch the Brandenburg Fifth if he sprang up and hurried, but he was too inert even to stir—to do anything except stay awake and on guard until Cal and Gun and Saul returned.

The shaded light at the head of his bed fluctuated a little, dimming, then brightening sharply, then dimming again as if the bulb were getting very old, but he was much too weary to get up and replace it or even just turn on another light. Besides, he didn't want his window too brightly lit for something on Corona Heights (Might still be there instead of here. Who knew?) to see.

He noted a faint, pale gray glitter around the edges of the casement window—the westering gibbous moon at last beginning to peer in from above, swing past the southern high rise into full view. He felt the impulse to get up and take a last look at the TV tower, say good night to his slender thousand-foot goddess attended by moon and stars, put her to bed, too, as it were, say his last prayers, but the same weariness prevented him. Also, he didn't want to show himself to Corona Heights or look upon the dark blotch of that place ever again.

The light at the head of his bed shone steadily, but it did seem a shade dimmer than it had been before the fluctuation, or was that just the pall cast by his evening mind?

Forget that now. Forget it all. The world was a rotten place. This city was a mess with its gimcrack high rises and trumpery skyscrapers—*Towers of Treason* indeed. It had all tumbled down and burned in 1906 (at least everything around this building had) and soon enough would again, and all of the papers be fed to the document-shredding machines, with or without the help of paramentals. (And was not humped, umber Corona Heights even now stirring?) And the entire world was just as bad; it was perishing of pollution, drowning and suffocating in chemical and atomic poisons, detergents and insecticides, industrial effluvia, smog, the stench of sulfuric acid, the quantities of steel, cement, aluminum ever bright, eternal plastics, omnipresent paper, gas and electron floods—electro-mephitic city-stuff indeed! though the world hardly needed the paranatural to do it to death. It was blackly cancerous, like Lovecraft's farm family slain by strange radioactives come by meteor from the end of nowhere.

But that was not the end. (He edged a little closer to his Scholar's Mistress.) The electro-mephitic sickness was spreading, had spread (had metastasized) from this world to everywhere. The universe was terminally diseased; it would die thermodynamically. Even the stars were infected. Who thought that those bright points of light meant anything? What were they but a swarm of phosphorescent fruit flies momentarily frozen in an utterly random pattern around a garbage planet?

He tried his best to "hear" the Brandenburg Fifth that Cal was playing, the vastly varied, infinitely ordered diamond streamers of quill-plucked sound that made it the parent of all piano concertos. Music has the power to release things, Cal had said, to make them fly. Perhaps it would break this mood. Papageno's bells were magic—and a protection against magic. But all was silence.

What was the use of life anyhow? He had laboriously recovered from his alcoholism only to face the Noseless

One once more in a new triangular mask. Effort wasted, he told himself. In fact, he would have reached out and taken a bitter, stinging drink from the square bottle, except he was too tired to make the effort. He was an old fool to think Cal cared for him, as much a fool as Byers with his camp Chinese swinger and his teen-agers, his kinky paradise of sexy, slim-fingered, groping cherubs.

Franz's gaze wandered to Daisy's painted, dark-nested face upon the wall, narrowed by perspective to slit eyes and mouth that sneered above a tapering chin.

At that moment he began to hear a very faint scuffing in the wall, like that of a very large rat trying very hard to be quiet. From how far did it come? He couldn't tell. What were the first sounds of an earthquake like?—the ones only the horses and dogs can hear. There came a louder scuff, then nothing more.

He remembered the relief he'd felt when cancer had lobotomized Daisy's brain and she had reached the presumably unfeeling vegetable stage ("the flat effect," neurologists called it as if the soaring house of mind became a lightless and low-ceilinged apartment complex) and the need to keep himself anesthetized with alcohol had become a shade less pressing.

The light behind his head arced brightly greenish white, fluttered, and went out. He started to sit up, but barely lifted a finger. The darkness in the room took forms like the Black Pictures of witchcraft, crowd-stupefying marvels, and Olympian horrors which Goya had painted for himself alone in his old age, a very proper way to decorate a home. His lifted finger vaguely moved toward Fernando's blacked-out star, then dropped back. A small sob formed and faded in his throat. He snuggled close to his Scholar's Mistress, his fingers touching her Lovecraftian shoulder. He thought of how she was the only real person that he had. Darkness and sleep closed on him without a sound.

Time passed.

Franz dreamed of utter darkness and of a great, white, crackling, ripping noise, as of endless sheets of newsprint being crumpled and dozens of books being torn across at once and their stiff covers cracked and crushed—a paper pandemonium.

But perhaps there was no mighty noise (only the sound of Time clearing her throat), for he next thought he woke very tranquilly into two rooms: this with the this-in-dream superimposed. He tried to make them come together. Daisy was lying peacefully beside him. Both he and she were very, very happy. They had talked last night and all was very well. Her slim, silken dry fingers touched his cheek and neck.

With a cold plunge of feelings, the suspicion came to him that she was dead. The touching fingers moved reassuringly. There seemed to be almost too many of them. No, Daisy was not dead, but she was very sick. She was alive, but in the vegetable stage, mercifully tranquilized by her malignancy. Horrible, yet it was still a comfort to lie beside her. Like Cal, she was so young, even in this half-death. Her fingers were so very slim and silken dry, so very strong and many, all starting to grip tightly—they were not fingers but wiry black vines rooted inside her skull, growing in profusion out of her cavernous orbits, gushing luxuriantly out of the triangular hole between the nasal and the vomer bones, twining in tendrils from under her upper teeth so white, pushing insidiously and insistently, like grass from sidewalk crack, out of her pale brown cranium, bursting apart the squamous, sagittal, and *coronal* sutures.

Franz sat up with a convulsive start, gagging on his feelings, his heart pounding, cold sweat breaking from his forehead.

28

MOONLIGHT WAS POURING in the casement window, making a long coffin-size pool upon the carpeted floor beyond the coffee table, throwing the rest of the room into darker shadow by contrast.

He was fully clothed; his feet ached in his shoes.

He realized with enormous gratitude that he was truly awake at last, that Daisy and the vegetative horror that had destroyed her were both gone, vanished far swifter than smoke.

He found himself acutely aware of all the space around him: the cool air against his face and hands, the eight chief corners of his room, the slot outside the window shooting down six floors between this building and the next to basement level, the seventh floor and roof above, the hall on the other side of the wall beyond the head of his bed, the broom closet on the other side of the wall beside him that held Daisy's picture and Fernando's star, and the airshaft beyond the broom closet.

And all his other sensations and all his thoughts seemed equally vivid and pristine. He told himself he had his morning mind again, all rinsed by sleep, fresh as sea air. How wonderful! He'd slept the whole night through (Had Cal and the boys knocked softly at his door and gone smiling and shrugging away?) and now waking an hour or so before dawn, just as the long astronomical twilight began, simply because he'd gone to sleep so early. Had Byers slept as well?—he doubted that, even with his skinny-slim, decadent soporifics.

But then he realized that the moonlight still was stream-

ing in, as it had started to do before he slept, proving that
he'd only been asleep an hour or less.

His skin quivered a little, and the muscles of his legs
grew tense, his whole body quickened as if in anticipation
of . . . he didn't know what.

He felt a paralyzing touch on the back of his neck. Then
the narrow, prickly dry vines (it felt—though they were
fewer now) moved with a faint rustle through his lifted
hairs past his ear to his right cheek and jaw. They were
growing out of the wall . . . no . . . they were not vines,
they were the fingers of the narrow right hand of his
Scholar's Mistress, who had sat up naked beside him, a
tall, pale shape unfeatured in the smudging gloom. She
had an aristocratically small, narrow face and head (black
hair?), a long neck, imperially wide shoulders, an elegant, Empire-high waist, slender hips, and long, long
legs—very much the shape of the skeletal steel TV tower,
a far slenderer Orion (with Rigel serving as a foot instead
of knee).

The fingers on her right arm that was snaked around his
neck now crept across his cheek and toward his lips, while
she turned and leaned her face a little toward his. It was
still featureless against the darkness, yet the question rose
unbidden in his mind whether it was just such an intense
look that the witch Asenath (Waite) Derby would have
turned upon her husband Edward Derby when they were
in bed, with old Ephraim Waite (Thibaut de Castries?)
peering with her from her hypnotic eyes.

She leaned her face closer still, the fingers of her right
hand crept softly yet intrusively upward toward his nostrils and eye, while out of the gloom at her left side her
other hand came weaving on its serpent-slender arm toward his face. All her movements and postures were
elegant and beautiful.

Shrinking away violently, he threw up his own left
hand protectively and with a convulsive thrust of his right
arm and of his legs against the mattress, he heaved his
body across the coffee table, oversetting it and carrying all
its heaped contents clattering and thudding and clashing

(the glasses and bottle and binoculars) and cascading with him to the floor beyond, where (having turned over completely) he lay in the edge of the pool of moonlight, except for his head, which was in the shadow between it and the door. In turning over, his face had come close to the big ashtray as it was oversetting and to the gushing kirschwasser bottle and he had gotten whiffs of stinking tobacco tar and stinging, bitter alcohol. He felt the hard shapes of chessmen under him. He was staring back wildly at the bed he'd quitted and for the moment he saw only darkness.

Then out of the darkness there lifted up, but not very high, the long, pale shape of his Scholar's Mistress. She seemed to look about her like a mongoose or weasel, her small head dipping this way and that on its slender neck; then with a nerve-racking dry rustling sound she came writhing and scuttling swiftly after him across the low table and all its scattered and disordered stuff, her long-fingered hands reaching out far ahead of her on their wiry pale arms. Even as he started to try to get to his feet, they closed upon his shoulder and side with a fearfully strong grip and there flashed instantaneously across his mind a remembered line of poetry—"Ghosts are we, but with skeletons of steel."

With a surge of strength born of his terror, he tore himself free of the trapping hands. But they had prevented him from rising, with the result that he had only heaved over again through the moonlit pool and lay on his back, threshing and flailing, in its far edge, his head still in shadow.

Papers and chessmen and the ashtray's contents scattered further and flew. A wineglass crunched as his heel hit it. The dumped phone began to beep like a furious pedantic mouse, from some near street a siren started to yelp like dogs being tortured, there was a great ripping noise as in his dream—the scattered papers churned and rose in seeming shreds a little from the floor—and through it all there sounded deep-throated, rasping screams which were Franz's own.

His Scholar's Mistress came twisting and hitching into the moonlight. Her face was still shadowed but he could see that *her thin, wide-shouldered body was apparently formed solely of shredded and tightly compacted paper*, mottled pale brown and yellowish with age, as if made up of the chewed pages of all the magazines and books that had formed her on the bed, while about and back from her shadowed face there streamed black hair. (The books' shredded black covers?) Her wiry limbs in particular seemed to be made up entirely of very tightly twisted and braided pale brown paper as she darted toward him with terrible swiftness and threw them around him, pinioning his own arms (and her long legs scissoring about his) despite all his flailings and convulsive kickings while, utterly winded by his screaming, he gasped and mewed.

Then she twisted her head around and up, so that the moonlight struck her face. It was narrow and tapering, shaped somewhat like a fox's or a weasel's, formed like the rest of her of fiercely compacted paper constrictedly humped and creviced, but layered over in this area with dead white (the rice paper?) speckled or pocked everywhere with a rash of irregular small black marks. (Thibaut's ink?) It had no eyes, although it seemed to stare into his brain and heart. It had no nose. (Was *this* the Noseless One?) It had no mouth—but then the long chin began to twitch and lift a little like a beast's snout and he saw that it was open at the end.

He realized that *this* was what had been under the loose robes and black veils of de Castries's Mystery Woman, who'd dogged his footsteps even to his grave, compact of intellectuality, all paper work (Scholar's Mistress indeed!), the Queen of the Night, the lurker at the summit, the thing that even Thibaut de Castries feared, Our Lady of Darkness.

The cables of the braided arms and legs twisted around him tighter and the face, going into shadow again, moved silently down toward his; and all that Franz could do was strain his own face back and away.

He thought in a flash of the disappearance of the gutted old pulp magazines and realized that they, crumbled and torn to bits, must have been the raw material for the pale brown figure in the casement window he'd seen twice from Corona Heights.

He saw on the black ceiling, above the dipping black-haired muzzle, a little patch of soft, harmonious ghostly colors—the pastel spectrum of moonlight, cast by one of his prisms lying in the pool on the floor.

The dry, rough, hard face pressed against his, blocking his mouth, squeezing his nostrils; the snout dug itself into his neck. He felt a crushing, incalculably great weight upon him. (The TV tower and the Transamerica! And the stars?) And filling his mouth and nose, the bone-dry, bitter dust of Thibaut de Castries.

At that instant the room was flooded with bright, white light and, as if it were an injected instant stimulant, he was able to twist his face away from the rugose horror and his shoulders halfway around.

The door to the hall was open wide, a key still in the lock, Cal was standing on the threshold, her back against the jamb, a finger of her right hand touching the light switch. She was panting, as if she'd been running hard. She was still wearing her white concert dress and over it her black velvet coat, hanging open. She was looking a little above and beyond him with an expression of incredulous horror. Then her finger dropped away from the light switch as her whole body slowly slid downward, bending only at the knees. Her back stayed very straight against the jamb, her shoulders were erect, her chin was high, her horror-filled eyes did not once blink. Then when she had gone down on her haunches, like a witch doctor, her eyes grew wider still with righteous anger, she tucked in her chin and put on her nastiest professional look, and in a harsh voice Franz had never heard her use before, she said:

"In the names of Bach, Mozart, and Beethoven, the names of Pythagoras, Newton, and Einstein, by Bertrand Russell, William James, and Eustace Hayden, begone!

All inharmonious and disorderly shapes and forces, depart at once!''

As she was speaking, the papers all around Franz (he could see now that they *were* shredded) lifted up cracklingly, the grips upon his arms and legs loosened, so that he was able to inch toward Cal while violently threshing his half-freed limbs. Midway in her eccentric exorcism, the pale shreds began to churn violently and suddenly were multiplied tenfold in numbers (all restrains on him as suddenly gone) so that, at the end he was crawling toward her through a thick paper snowstorm.

The innumerable-seeming shreds sank rustlingly all around him to the floor. He laid his head in her lap where she now sat erect in the doorway, half-in, half-out, and he lay there gasping, one hand clutching her waist, the other thrown out as far as he could reach into the hallway as if to mark on the carpet the point of farthest advance. He felt Cal's reassuring fingers on his cheek, while her other hand absently brushed scraps of paper from his coat.

29

FRANZ HEARD GUN say urgently, "Cal, are you all right? Franz!" Then Saul; "What the hell's happened to his room?" Then Gun again; "My God, it looks like his whole library's been put to the Destroysit!" but all that Franz could see of them were shoes and legs. How odd. There was a third pair—brown denim pants, and scuffed brown shoes, rather small; of course—Fernando.

Doors opened down the hall and heads thrust out. The elevator doors opened and Dorotea and Bonita hurried out, their faces anxious and eager. But what Franz found himself looking at, because it really puzzled him, was a score or more of dusty corrugated cartons neatly piled along the wall of the hall opposite the broom closet, and with them three old suitcases and a small trunk.

Saul had knelt down beside him and was professionally touching his wrist and chest, drawing back his eyelids with a light touch to check the pupils, not saying anything. Then he nodded reassuringly to Cal.

Franz managed an inquiring look. Saul smiled at him easily and said, "You know, Franz, Cal left that concert like a bat out of hell. She took her bows with the other soloists and she waited for the conductor to take his, but then she grabbed up her coat—she'd brought it onstage during the second intermission and laid it on the bench beside her (I'd given her your message)—and she took off straight through the audience. You thought *you'd* offended 'em by leaving at the start. Believe me, it was nothing to the way she treated 'em! By the time we caught sight of her again, she was stopping a taxi by running out into the

street in front of it. If we'd have been a bit slower, she'd
have ditched us. As it was, she grudged us the time it took
us to get in.''

"And then she got ahead of us again when we each
thought the other would pay the cab driver and he yelled at
us and we both went back," Gun took up over his shoulder from where he stood inside the room at the edge of the
great drift of shredded paper and stuff, as if hesitant to
disturb it. "When we got inside she'd run up the stairs. By
then the elevator had come down, so we took it, but she
beat us anyway. Say, Franz," he asked, pointing, "Who
chalked that big star on your wall over the bed?''

At that question, Franz saw the small brown scuffed
shoes step out decisively, kicking through the paper
snow. Once again Fernando loudly rapped the wall above
the bed, as if for attention, and turned and said authorita-
tively, "*Hechiceria ocultado en muralla!*"

"Witchcraft hidden in the wall," Franz translated,
rather like a child trying to prove he's not sick. Cal
touched his lips reprovingly, he should rest.

Fernando lifted a finger, as if to announce, "I will
demonstrate," and came striding back, stepping carefully
past Cal and Franz in the doorway. He went quickly down
the hall past Dorotea and Bonita, and stopped in front of
the broom closet door and turned around. Gun, who had
followed inquisitively behind him, stopped, too.

The dark Peruvian gestured from the shut doorway to
the neatly stacked boxes twice and then took a couple of
steps on his toes with knees bent. ("I moved them out. I
did it quietly.") and took a big screwdriver out of his
pants pocket and thrust it into the hole where the knob had
been and gave it a twist and with it drew the black door
open and then with a peremptory flourish of the screwdriver stepped inside.

Gun followed and looked in, reporting back to Franz
and Cal, "He's got the whole little room cleared out. My
God, it's dusty. You know, it's even got a little window.
Now he's kneeling by the wall that's the other side of the
one he pounded on. There's a little shallow cupboard built

into it low down. It's got a door. Fuses? Cleaning stuff?
Outlets? I don't know. Now he's using the screwdriver to
pry it open. Well, I'll be damned!''

He backed away to let Fernando emerge, smiling triumphantly and carrying before his chest a rather large, rather
thin gray book. He knelt by Franz and held it out to him,
dramatically opening it. There was a puff of dust.

The two pages randomly revealed were covered from
top to bottom, Franz saw, with unbroken lines of neatly
yet crabbedly inked black astronomical and astrological
signs and other cryptic symbols.

Franz reached out shakily toward it, then jerked his
hand sharply back, as though afraid of getting his fingers
burned.

He recognized the hand that had penned the Curse.

It had to be the Fifty-Book, the Grand Cipher mentioned in *Megapolisomancy* and Smith's journal (B)—the
ledger that Smith had once seen and that was an essential
ingredient (A) of the Curse and that had been hidden
almost forty years ago by old Thibaut de Castries to do its
work at the fulcrum (0) at (Franz shuddered, glancing up
at the number on his door) 607 Rhodes.

30

NEXT DAY GUN incinerated the Grand Cipher at Franz's urgent entreaty, Cal and Saul concurring, but only after microfilming it. Since then he'd fed it to his computers repeatedly and let several semanticists and linguists study it variously, without the least progress toward breaking the code, if there is one. Recently he told the others, "It almost looks like Thibaut de Castries may have created that mathematical will-o'-the-wisp—a set of completely random numbers." There did turn out to be exactly fifty symbols. Cal pointed out that fifty was the total number of faces of all the five Pythagorean or Platonic solids. But when asked what that led to, she could only shrug.

At first Gun and Saul couldn't help wondering whether Franz mightn't have torn up all his books and papers in some sort of short-term psychotic seizure. But they concluded it would have been an impossible task, at least to do in so short a time. "That stuff was shredded like oakum."

Gun kept some samples of the strange confetti—"irregular scraps, average width three millimeters"—nothing like the refuse of a document-shredding machine, however advanced. (Which seemed to dispose of the suspicion that Gun's Shredbasket, or some other supersubtle Italianate machinery, had somehow played a part in the affair.)

Gun also took apart Franz's binoculars (calling in his optical friend, who among other things had investigated and thoroughly debunked the famous Crystal Skull) but they found no trace of any gimmicking. The only noteworthy circumstance was the thoroughness with which the lenses and prisms had been smashed. "More oakum picking?"

Gun found one flaw in the detailed account Franz gave when he was up to it. "You simply can't see spectral colors in moonlight. The cones of the retina aren't that sensitive."

Franz replied somewhat sharply, "Most people can never see the green flash of the setting sun. Yet it's sometimes there."

Saul's comment was, "You've got to believe there's some sort of sense in everything that crazies say."

"Crazies?"

"All of us."

He and Gun still live at 811 Geary. They've encountered no further paramental phenomena—at least as yet.

The Luques are still there, too. Dorotea is keeping the existence of the broom closets a secret, especially from the owner of 811. "He'd make me e-try to rent them if he knew."

Fernando's story, as finally interpreted by her and Cal, was simply that he'd once noticed the little, low, very shallow cupboard in the broom closet while rearranging the boxes there to make space for additional ones and that it had stuck in his mind (*"Misterioso!"*) so that when *"Meestair Juestón"* had become haunted, he had remembered it and played a hunch. The cupboard, by the stains on its bottom, had once held polishes for furniture, brass, and shoes, but then for almost forty years only the Fifty-Book.

The three Luques and the others (nine in all with Gun's and Saul's ladies—just the right number for a classic Roman party, Franz observed) did eventually go for a picnic on Corona Heights. Gunnar's Ingrid was tall and blonde as he, and worked in the Environmental Protection Agency, and pretended to be greatly impressed by the Junior Museum. While Saul's Joey was a red-haired little dietitian deep into community theater. The Heights seemed quite different now that the winter's rains had turned it green. Yet there were surprising reminders of a

grimmer period: they encountered the two little girls with
the Saint Bernard. Franz went a shade pale at that, but
rallied quickly. Bonita played with them a while, nicely
pretending it was fun. All in all, they had an enjoyable
time, but no one sat in the Bishop's Seat or hunted beneath
it for signs of an old interment. Franz remarked afterward,
"I sometimes think the injunction not to move old bones
is at the root of all the para . . . supernatural."

He tried to get in touch with Jaime Byers again, but
phone calls and even letters went unanswered. Later he
learned that the affluent poet and essayist, accompanied
by Fa Lo Suee (and Shirl Soames too, apparently), had
gone for an extended trip around the world.

"Somebody always does that at the end of a supernatural horror story," he commented sourly, with slightly
forced humor. "*The Hound of the Baskervilles*, etcetera.
I'd really like to know who his sources were besides Klaas
and Ricker. But perhaps it's just as well I don't get into
that."

He and Cal now share an apartment a little farther up
Nob Hill. Though they haven't married, Franz swears
he'll never live alone again. He never slept another night
in Room 607.

As to what Cal heard and saw (and did) at the end, she
says, "When I got to the third floor I heard Franz start to
scream. I had his key out. There were all those bits of
paper swirling around him like a whirlpool. But at its
center they hugged him and made a sort of tough, skinny
pillar with a nasty top. So I said (*pace* my father) the first
things that came into my mind. The pillar flew apart like a
Mexican *piñata* and became part of the paper storm,
which settled down very quickly, like snowflakes on the
moon. You know, it was inches deep. As soon as I had got
Franz's message from Saul, I'd known I must get to him
as quickly as I could, but only after we'd played the
Brandenburg."

Franz thinks the Brandenburg Fifth somehow saved
him, along with Cal's subsequent quick action, but as to

how, he has no theories. Cal says about that only, "I think it's fortunate that Bach had a mathematical mind and that Pythagoras was musical."

Once, in a picky mood, she speculated, "You know, the talents attributed to de Castries's 'father's young Polish mistress' (and his mystery lady?) would correspond quite exactly with those of a being made up entirely of shredded multilingual occult books: amazing command of languages, learned beyond measure in the weird, profound secretarial skills, a tendency to fly apart like an explosive doll, black polka-dotted veil of crape and all— all merciless night animal, yet with a wisdom that goes back to Egypt, an erotic virtuoso (really, I'm a bit jealous), great grasp of culture and art—"

"Far too strong a grasp!" Franz cut her short with a shudder.

But Cal pressed on, a shade maliciously, "And then the way you caressed her intimately from head to heels and made lovey talk to her before you fell asleep—no wonder she became aroused!"

"I always knew we'd be found out some day." He tried to pass it off with a joke, but his hand shook a little as he lit a cigarette.

For a while after that Franz was very particular about never letting a book or magazine stay on the bed. But just the other day Cal found a straggling line of three there, on the side nearest the wall. She didn't touch them, but she did tell him about it. "I don't know if I could swing it again," she said. "So take care."

Cal says, "Everything's very chancy."

Fantasy from Ace
fanciful and fantastic!

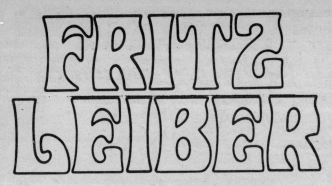

FRITZ LEIBER

FAFHRD AND THE GRAY MOUSER SAGA

☐ 79179-4	**SWORDS AND DEVILTRY**	$2.75
☐ 79158-1	**SWORDS AGAINST DEATH**	$2.75
☐ 79188-3	**SWORDS IN THE MIST**	$2.75
☐ 79187-5	**SWORDS AGAINST WIZARDRY**	$2.75
☐ 79227-8	**THE SWORDS OF LANKHMAR**	$2.75
☐ 79189-1	**SWORDS AND ICE MAGIC**	$2.75

Prices may be slightly higher in Canada.

BEST-SELLING
Science Fiction
and
Fantasy

☐ 47809-3	**THE LEFT HAND OF DARKNESS,** Ursula K. LeGuin	$2.95
☐ 16012-3	**DORSAI!,** Gordon R. Dickson	$2.75
☐ 80581-7	**THIEVES' WORLD,** Robert Lynn Asprin, editor	$2.95
☐ 11577-2	**CONAN #1,** Robert E. Howard, L. Sprague de Camp, Lin Carter	$2.50
☐ 49142-1	**LORD DARCY INVESTIGATES,** Randell Garrett	$2.75
☐ 21889-X	**EXPANDED UNIVERSE,** Robert A. Heinlein	$3.95
☐ 87328-6	**THE WARLOCK UNLOCKED,** Christopher Stasheff	$2.95
☐ 26187-6	**FUZZY SAPIENS,** H. Beam Piper	$2.75
☐ 05469-2	**BERSERKER,** Fred Saberhagen	$2.75
☐ 10253-0	**CHANGELING,** Roger Zelazny	$2.95
☐ 51552-5	**THE MAGIC GOES AWAY,** Larry Niven	$2.75

Prices may be slightly higer in Canada.

Available at your local bookstore or return this form to:

ACE SCIENCE FICTION
Book Mailing Service
P.O. Box 690, Rockville Centre, NY 11571

Please send me the titles checked above. I enclose _____ Include 75¢ for postage and handling if one book is ordered; 25¢ per book for two or more not to exceed $1.75. California, Illinois, New York and Tennessee residents please add sales tax.

NAME_____

ADDRESS_____

CITY_____STATE/ZIP_____

(allow six weeks for delivery)

SF 9